W9-ATS-785

Local News

with Connections

Also by Gary Soto in HRW LIBRARY:

Béisbol en abril y otras historias

Local News

Gary Soto

with Connections

HOLT, RINEHART AND WINSTON

A Harcourt Classroom Education Company

Austin · New York · Orlando · Atlanta · San Francisco · Boston · Dallas · Toronto · London

For permission to reprint copyrighted material, grateful acknowledgment is made to the following sources:

Harcourt, Inc.: *Local News* by Gary Soto. Copyright © 1993 by Gary Soto.

Asian American Studies Center, University of California, Los Angeles: "Through Anger and Love" from *The Chauvinist and Other Stories* by Toshio Mori. Copyright © 1979 by The Regents of the University of California. **Merlyn's Pen, Inc.:** "Taking Off" by Kristen Binck from *Taking Off and Other Coming of Age Stories,* edited by Kathryn Kulpa. Copyright © by Merylyn's Pen, Inc. **Naomi Shihab Nye:** "The Use of Fiction" by Naomi Shihab Nye from *Antaeus.* Copyright © by Naomi Shihab Nye.

Cover Credit: Photographs: (people) Sam Dudgeon/HRW Photo; (newspaper) Victoria Smith/HRW Photo. Layout: Curtis Riker, Chris Smith.

Printed in the United States of America

ISBN 0-03-066074-2

5 6   043   05 04

For Gerald Haslam, local boy

Contents

CONTINUED

Connections

Local News

bLACKMAIL

LIKE MOST OF HIS FRIENDS at school, Angel had an older, mean brother who pushed him around and played dirty tricks on him. One time his brother, Javier, nicknamed "Little Weasel" because he had a long, skinny neck, stuck Angel's bike up in the tree. With the help of his *vato loco* friends, all laughing and spitting sunflower seeds, Weasel hauled the bike to the top of the palm tree that stood in front of their pink stucco house.

"Get it down, Weasel!" Angel screamed, fists clenched and upper lip quivering from anger.

"You accusing me, *ese?*" his brother said, laughing. He spat on the ground and said, "Swim in it, *ese.*"

Javier did not take the bike down until their *papi* drove his squeaky truck into the driveway. Their father, a carpenter, didn't like dealing with arguing kids when he came home from work, tired from whacking nails for eight hours.

Another time, when Angel was real young, just out of the stroller, Little Weasel purposefully lost him at the Fresno Fair. Weasel snuck away on noiseless Air Jordans, and when Angel turned around, his face sticky with cotton candy, his brother was out of sight. Tears welled up in Angel's eyes and his mouth pulled down like a fish's. He wandered through hordes of people, crying, "Weasel, where are you?", a torrent of tears sprinkling his cotton candy. When Angel stopped a woman and asked if she had seen Weasel, she pointed to a tall white building and said, "Check the farm animals."

There had been other tricks. Early one summer morning, Angel had gone out to get the newspaper, and when he returned, shooting the rubber band at their cat, Pleitos, the front door clicked shut and Weasel's laughing *cara* appeared at the window. Angel was locked out, with only his pajama bottoms on.

"Let me in!" Angel screamed at the smirking Weasel, who cupped a hand around an ear and mouthed, "What? I can't hear you, *carnal*."

Angel spent the day hiding in the garage until his parents came home from work.

Weasel was sneaky. One day he had tiptoed into the bathroom. Angel was in the shower, a *bigote* of soapsuds under each arm. Weasel yanked back the shower curtain, said, "Cheese, *ese*," and took a Polaroid picture before Angel could cover himself with a washcloth. He just stood there, naked as the day he was born, his mouth hanging open in shock.

Weasel threatened his brother, waving the picture in front of him. "Twenty bucks by tomorrow or the *rucas*, the girls at school, are gonna get to see that you look like a plucked chicken."

Weasel laughed as he hurried out of the bathroom, leaving Angel with soap under each arm and some in his eyes.

"You punk!" Angel screamed. "I'm gonna get you!"

Angel rinsed off and climbed out of the shower, pink as a crab. He dressed quickly, pulling up his pants as he ran into the living room. "Where are you?" Angel screamed. He zipped his zipper and pulled his arms through a T-shirt splashed with a picture of Los Lobos.

He checked their bedroom, the kitchen, their parents' bedroom, and every crammed closet. Weasel had disappeared like smoke. Angel mumbled a litany of threats and cuss words and stomped outside to the front yard, where Pleitos was sleeping in a puddle of sunlight.

"Where are you, Weasel?" Angel called from their lawn while he scanned the neighborhood. There was no one in sight along the street except their neighbor, Mr. Mendoza, who was sprinkling fertilizer on his dead lawn.

"Have you seen Weasel?" Angel asked Mr. Mendoza, who shook his head. Angel sighed, returned to the front porch, stroked his cat, and asked, "Where did Weasel go?"

Pleitos looked up, a snaggle tooth jutting from the

corner of his mouth, and took a swat at Angel's hand.

"*Ay!*" Angel screamed, sucking his scratched hand. He rapped Pleitos's head with a knuckle. "You're a bad *gato!* No wonder the other cats don't like you."

Just then Weasel rode by on his bike. He waved the snapshot at Angel and yelled, "Twenty bucks, dude. I know you got it."

Angel jumped off the porch and started after his brother, who rode just fast enough so Angel couldn't catch him.

"Come on, man," Angel begged, sneakers slapping against the asphalt. "Let me have it!"

"Twenty bucks, man."

"I don't got it," panted Angel.

"You do, too. Your *nina* sent you something for your birthday."

"It was only five dollars," Angel said as he slowed down, out of breath.

Weasel circled on the bike and said, "That's too bad. It's gonna be show-and-tell, *ese*."

"Come on, Weasel, I'm your brother."

"That's why I'm doing it to you. I can't do this to my friends."

Weasel popped a wheelie and rode away. Angel returned to the house, sweaty as a horse. But he didn't dare get back into the shower. There was no telling when Weasel might return, next time with a video camera, maybe.

"I could have at least had on my *chones*," Angel lamented. But no, he'd been naked, and now it seemed he would have to leave town or die from embarrassment. Weasel always followed through with his threats.

After a moment of deep thought, Angel snapped his fingers and shouted, "I got it!" He ran inside the house and brought out the photo albums, recalling a baby photograph of Weasel standing in the buff by a blow-up pool. He flipped through the plastic pages. When he finally spotted the snapshot, creased and dirty, he cried, "Bingo! I'm saved!" He took it from the plastic sleeve and laughed at the photograph of a two-year-old baby with arms fat as water balloons. It was Weasel, all right. Both fists were clenched and raised, ready to fight, and a candy cigarette was hanging from the corner of his mouth.

"I'll get that punk now!" Angel said, slipping the picture into his back pocket. It's my turn to blackmail, he thought, nursing a glass of soda while he waited on the couch for his brother.

When Weasel returned home, hot and tired from popping wheelies, he ripped the soda from Angel's hand and took a long swig, spitting an ice cube back into the glass.

"Did Louie call?" Weasel asked as he handed the soda back to Angel.

"I don't want the soda no more. You ruined it with your lips," Angel scolded. "But I got you now, Weasel!"

Javier ignored his brother and went into the kitchen to help himself to a thick peanut-butter tortilla. He stopped chewing just long enough to clear his throat and ask Angel if he was sure that Louie hadn't called.

"You're not listening, Weasel."

"I am," he answered, taking another bite of tortilla. He leaned against the kitchen counter, savoring his snack.

"I have your baby picture, the one when you were naked," Angel taunted, patting the pocket where he had stashed the photo. "You didn't have your *chones* on."

"So?"

"I'll show it to your friends!" Angel's eyes were lit with excitement. He thought he'd cornered his brother.

"*Pues*, it's no big deal, *carnal*."

"Yeah? Well, I'm gonna show it to Vicky!"

Weasel stopped chewing and thought for a moment, his eyes raised toward the ceiling. "Yeah," he said, swallowing a lump of tortilla. "Do me a favor and show it to Vicky. She's mad at me. It might perk her up to see me when I was *un esquincle*."

Angel flopped his arms at his sides. It's not working, he thought. He scolded his brother, "You're bad, man. You're gonna end up in juvie."

Weasel laughed and went to the living room. He turned on the television, propped his feet on his father's hassock, and watched the Giants thrash the Astros, 15–5.

Angel argued with him all afternoon.

"I'm gonna hurt you," Angel said.

"You and the *policía?*"

"I'm gonna take your watch, Weasel!"

"It's broken."

"I know where you keep your money."

"I spent it."

"I'm gonna tell Grandpa!"

"He's hard of hearing."

"I'm gonna tell Raymond. He can beat you up."

"Sorry, dude. He's in juvie."

Angel ran out of threats and Weasel was still hungry. He got up, hopped to the kitchen, and stuffed a handful of lunch meat into his mouth. He chewed, swallowed, wiped his mouth on the back of his hand, and began to reason with his brother.

"If you want this picture back," he said, touching his shirt pocket, "you're gonna have to work for me."

"Like what?" Angel saw a crack of hope.

"Like dishes. Like washing Dad's truck. I'm supposed to do it." Weasel opened the refrigerator and took a swig from an opened half-liter of soda.

"You're not supposed to drink from the bottle, Weasel," Angel said. "You can spread germs."

"My germs are cute, man. That's what Vicky says." Weasel took a long swig, his Adam's apple riding up and down. He smacked his lips and said, "*¿Entiendes?* You pick up the slack this week, and I'll give you this photo in a jiffy." He took out the snapshot and laughed. "You look like a worm, Homes."

Angel thought for a moment. His brother had tricked him before. He could do it again. But Angel didn't see any other way out. He couldn't risk going to school and finding himself tacked on the fourth-grade bulletin board next to Current Affairs.

"OK, you're the boss," Angel agreed. "But you better give it to me. You promise?"

"Scout's honor," Weasel said, holding one hand up.

They slapped palms, and Angel got busy right away

7

cleaning their bedroom and scrubbing the toilet, Weasel's job that week. Then he ironed all of Weasel's white T-shirts and khakis. He polished Weasel's bike, working a sock through the spokes until they shone like knives.

Dinner that night was a clatter of happy noise. Their father was happy because he had been moved from right field to second base, a sign of respect, he thought. He played softball for Azteca Construction, but he had barely made the team. He had been helped into the infield by three misfortunes—a sprained ankle for "Spider," a pulled groin for Pedro, and for Leonard, "El Gordo," a drunken driving rap with no license, no insurance, and one headlight gone.

"You should have seen me snatch that pop-up the other night," their father said, beaming, his face fat with *frijoles*. Placing his fork on his plate, he raised his hands and looked toward the ceiling. He popped one fist into the flat of his other palm and shouted to his imaginary teammates, "I got it. Step back. I'm the hero, man."

"Pop-ups are easy," said Weasel.

"Not this one. It was so high it came down roasted."

"Dad, it was probably just a little dinky one like I used to catch with my plastic mitt."

"Hey, *mocoso*, you talkin' trash to your *papi?*"

Then Weasel asked if there were any girls on the team.

"*¿Qué?*" their father snapped, his eyes angry.

"I'm jus' askin'. It's nothin' personal, *Papi*. You know some of these *rucas* are really good, better than us *vatos*."

He looked at their mother, who was reading a magazine. "Mom, did I say anything wrong?"

For his rudeness, Weasel was assigned to pull the weeds in the flower bed.

"I want them out by the time I get back!" their father said.

"Where you goin'?" Angel asked.

"To play ball."

After their father left, Weasel snapped his fingers at Angel and said, "You can start now."

"What?"

"Start weedin', Homes. I'm going to the playground to check out the girls."

"But Dad said for you to do it," Angel shouted. He stomped toward Weasel, who pushed him away and started combing his hair in front of the hall mirror. He bared his teeth at the mirror and scraped his front teeth with a fingernail.

"It's not fair, Weasel. Dad said for *you* to pull the weeds."

Weasel turned his head toward his brother, patted his shirt pocket, and smiled. "Be cool, dude."

So Angel spent the last hour of daylight pulling up tangles of yellowish weeds, while Pleitos sat on the lawn, blinking from sleepiness. Angel's arms ached, and a dime-sized blister rose on one palm. He was as bored as a convict and full of self-pity when he looked up to see his friends throwing dirt clods at each other nearby. It looked like fun.

Still, he kept pulling weeds. He couldn't risk his brother passing the snapshot around at school.

Later that night, when their father returned home limping, Weasel was waiting on the front porch to greet him. He apologized for having spoken rudely at dinner.

"*Papi*, look how I fixed up the flower bed."

The father looked at the finished work. He nodded, impressed, though he seemed more concerned about his pain.

"Did you hurt yourself?"

"*Simón*. I slid into second and burned my *nalgas*."

"Were you safe or out?"

"I was out. And they moved me back to right field."

"*Qué lástima, Papi*. I've felt that before. Rejection!" He spit a mouthful of sunflower seed shells into the flower bed. "It hurts right here," he said, touching his heart.

The father told Weasel to be quiet, that he was breaking the camel's back with his talk. He turned to Angel, who was standing between them. The boy's face was flushed from the strain of weeding, and his T-shirt was as dirty as a dish rag.

"You been playin' in the mud, Angel?" the father asked.

"He's been scratchin' around with the chickens, *qué no?*" Weasel said. "The dude's got lice."

Angel glared at his brother. He had had enough. "Dad, Weasel's tryin' to pull something on me. He's got—"

"*Cállate*, Homes," Weasel warned, spraying another mouthful of shells into the flower bed.

"He's got a picture of me——"

"Yeah, I got a picture of my little brother in my wallet. He means so much to me, the little *piojo*."

Their father waved them off, calling them two *chistosos*, and limped inside the house to shower, get into bed, and hope that his burned *nalgas* would feel better in the morning.

After his father left, Weasel turned to Angel and said, "I thought we had a deal, Homes?"

"You're mean," Angel said under his breath.

"*¿Yo?*" Weasel said, feigning surprise and pointing a finger at his chest. "*¿Yo?* I'm a good bro'. I'm just teaching you about life, about *la vida*, Homes.

"Look." Weasel brought out his wallet and thrust a picture of Madonna in Angel's face. *"Es mi ruca."*

Angel took the wallet and gazed at Madonna, a picture cut from a magazine. Her image faced a picture of Weasel, with a real cigarette between his teeth.

Angel handed the wallet back. "She ain't your girlfriend."

"Hey, Homes, use good grammar when you talk about my baby."

"She don't know you."

"*Pues, sí.* She likes to kiss me." Giggling, Weasel closed the wallet so that Madonna's face pressed against his face. He opened and closed it nine times and said, "OK, Madonna, no more. I'm tired of kissin'."

Angel had to laugh. *Qué loco*, he thought. What a crazy brother.

11

"And she likes you, too," Weasel told Angel. "She's got a crush on you. She told me to tell you that you're the real thing." He removed his picture from the wallet and replaced it with the Polaroid snapshot of Angel in the shower.

Angel and Weasel laughed as Weasel opened and closed the wallet, Madonna's face falling against Angel's snapshot.

"Oh, you're so cute," Weasel said, imitating Madonna's voice. "Don't kiss so hard, little Angel. You're hurtin' me."

The two brothers laughed, and Angel tried it himself, flapping the wallet open and closed. "Angel, you're so handsome, *pero* your brother *es tan feo.*"

They laughed and punched each other playfully. The game was over. Weasel flicked the snapshot at Angel; it brushed his forehead and landed on the porch. Pleitos, who had sauntered around the corner, sniffed at the snapshot. Angel pushed the cat away and picked the photo up.

"It's yours, dude," Weasel said, boxing with Pleitos.

"Thanks, Weasel."

"*Simón,*" he called, disappearing into the house.

Under the orange glare of the porch light, Angel studied the snapshot closely. He couldn't believe that that naked boy in the shower was him. The figure was dark, blurry, with hair plastered down and ears big as baseball mitts. Was his brother tricking him again? he wondered.

He showed it to Pleitos, who was rubbing his hard head against Angel's leg. "Does that look like me?"

Pleitos seemed to look intently at the snapshot. He looked and then, mean as ever, shot a quick jab at the snapshot. So Pleitos had recognized him. Only then did Angel know that it was really him—dripping water and shame, naked as a plucked chicken.

TRICK-OR-TREATING

ALMA WENT TRICK-OR-TREATING for the first time when she was two years old, waddling from house to house, ducklike, in her diaper. Her two older brothers tugged her along and fed her bites of candy at each stop. She was dressed as Baby Huey, an easy costume because she already had the diaper hanging from her hips and a yellow baby blanket to drape over one shoulder. She shook her plastic rattle, drooled, and smiled at the people who rained candies and dimes into her shopping bag and gushed, "Oh, how cute she is."

The next year she skipped Halloween because of chicken pox, which she had caught from her brother Ricky, who had gotten the virus from their brother, Manuel, who had picked it up from someone at school. But in her fourth year Alma was once again Baby Huey. People dropped candies into her crinkled paper bag, along with dimes and apples and a couple of bananas. She gave the treats to her grandmother, who in turn gave them to the police to X-ray (or ray-X, as she would say). They were clear of any foreign objects, and the next day one of the bananas, sliced thin so it could be shared by four children, floated in the morning cereal.

As the years passed Alma became even more thrilled about dressing up on Halloween. One year she went trick-or-treating as a princess, with a crown of aluminum foil sparkling on her head. The next year she was Frankenstein, with corks glued to her temples by her brothers and two painted cardboard boxes for shoes. Another year she went as a ghost, which was as easy as being Baby Huey because all she had to do to get showered with candies was wrap her bedsheet around herself and say "Boo!"

Now thirteen, and on her own for Halloween because her brothers had left for college, Alma was still thrilled about trick-or-treating. She parted the curtain and looked out the window. Darkness was creeping like a cat up the street. A few toothless jack-o'-lanterns flickered with orange light from front porches. The wind shook the trees, loosening a few stubborn leaves.

"What are you going to be?" Alma's mother asked. Already in her robe, she was filling a bowl with jaw-breakers and sticks of gum. Alma was embarrassed that her mother always gave away cheap candy, and never the good things like Milky Ways, Nerds, or boxes of Junior Mints. She gave it away stingily, too. Each kid who knocked on the door got only one candy, never a fistful.

"A football player," Alma said.

15

"¿Qué?"

"I'm using Manuel's old helmet and pads."

Both her brothers had played football for Roosevelt High School and they had each worn the same pads and helmet. Neither of the boys was a good player; they often came home with dark bruises. But playing football had been something to weigh their shoulders down with memory. Manuel, the middle brother, at age twenty-two was already a booster for Roosevelt High, and Ricky, the oldest, who had graduated from USC, sat glued to the TV every Saturday and Sunday watching college football.

Alma went to her bedroom, where she strapped on the pads and then slipped the jersey over her head, working it around so that it draped to the tops of her thighs like a mini-skirt. She pulled on the helmet, the strap dangling like a loose Band-Aid.

"Hello," she said, and the word boomed inside the helmet. She yelled "Trick or treat!" so loudly her eardrums hurt.

Alma returned to the living room just as her father was coming in the door. He was tired from work, and the stubble on his face was the color of iron filings.

"Hey, Dad," she said, bending over in a football stance.

For a minute, he looked at his daughter inquisitively. Then he asked, "Is that you, Manuel?"

"No, it's me," Alma said, standing up and pulling off the helmet. She gave her father a big, sweet smile and then led him like a little boy to his chair, where he plopped down with a sigh.

"I'm going trick-or-treating," Alma said. "I'm gonna skip dinner."

Her father couldn't help himself. "Aren't you gettin' a little too old, *mi'ja?*"

"It's my last year, Dad," she said, pushing the pumpkin-sized helmet back onto her head. "Manuel and Ricky went trick-or-treating until they were seventeen. Don't you remember?"

Her father didn't say anything. He yawned a wide, sleepy yawn and zapped on the TV.

It was true that all of Alma's friends at school had given up going trick-or-treating. They stayed home and complained that life was boring and that there was nothing to do except paint their fingernails and read their boyfriends' letters over and over. Alma didn't envy her friends on Halloween. After all, her fingernails were stubs and she hated boys. She went to the kitchen and gave her mother a birdlike peck on the cheek. "I'll be back early."

Her mother was at the stove frying round steak. "Be careful," she warned. "Don't eat anything that's not wrapped."

"I won't," Alma said as she left by the back door. Her cat, Tootsie Roll, sat on the hood of the Chevy Nova, a car that had been sitting in their driveway for two years. Her father planned to restore it. Spiderwebs dangled from the tires, and rust spots were beginning to pop up like pimples.

"Hey, you lazy thing," Alma said as she ran a hand through the cat's fur. Tootsie Roll stood, arching his back and yawning, and then poked his nose curiously at Alma's paper bag. She petted her cat and then hurried off to go trick-or-treating.

Alma ran up Mrs. Gonzalez's porch steps in three leaps. She rapped on the door, and Mrs. Gonzalez, wrapped in a housedress printed with splashes of stars and orange moons, unlocked the screen door and smiled.

"*Ay,* my pretty one," Mrs. Gonzalez said, her lined face bunching with happiness. She reached into her bag and brought out a syrupy popcorn ball wrapped in cellophane, the same treat she always gave. "You gettin' so big."

Alma breathed deeply behind the helmet. "Thank you."

"And how is your mommy?"

"Fine."

"Your daddy?"

"Fine. I'll tell them 'hi' for you."

Alma waved good-bye and leapt carelessly from the porch. She believed that if she crashed, the cushion of the helmet and pads would keep her from getting hurt. She landed with a thud, rolled gently, and got up brushing grass from her jersey.

Alma worked her way up the street, stopping only at the houses where she was sure to get good candy. Her Safeway shopping bag soon became heavy. When she ran from one house to the next, the candies rattled inside her bag and the pads on her shoulders flapped like wings.

"Trick or treat!" she yelled, standing with a clot of little kids. The little kids each got one candy, but Alma grabbed two or three, her eyes always spotting the best candy in the bunch.

Things were different at a house where a man in a dirty T-shirt thrust a bowl of walnuts at her. She took the walnuts, examining them closely, and then looked up at the man. His smile was the smile of a smashed jack-o'-lantern—all but two teeth were gone.

"What are you supposed to be? Roger Craig?" he giggled. His belly jiggled under his T-shirt. His fat son came to look at Alma, who hurried away with a feeble "thank you."

When she was out of sight of the odd man and his son, Alma tossed the walnuts in the gutter, took off her helmet, and unwrapped a Tootsie Roll, which she ate while thinking of her sleepyhead cat. Her face was hot from having been encased for so long in hard plastic.

She looked around. There were few trick-or-treaters on the street, certainly none her age. Most were little kids dragging bags, or mothers with flashlights pointing a safe path for the children.

Alma went from house to house and at almost every stop, she hovered among kids, some of whom were so young they couldn't talk.

"They're so slow," Alma muttered to herself. She felt she was losing time. The little kids held out their bags and looked dully at their treats. Their faces were smeared with chocolate. They were getting in her way. Little brats, she thought, they should be in bed.

But her feelings changed quickly. As she was leaving one house where she had gotten only a stick of gum, she saw a heavyset kid in an L.A. Raiders jacket snatch a bag from a little Ninja Turtle.

Irate, Alma raced after the big kid, who was about her age. The football helmet bounced loosely on her head, and the pads flapped up and down on her shoulders. She ran after the candy-snatcher, knees pumping high, and when she was almost on him, when she could grip his jacket, she leapt and tackled him. The boy kicked and struggled. He tried to smack Alma but instead hurt his knuckles on the hard helmet. And when he tried to knee her, she rammed a shoulder pad into his stomach, which quieted him. The kid gasped and rolled into a ball, groaning.

"You creep!" she yelled, undoing her chin strap and pulling off the helmet. She got to her feet and glared at the little kids who had come running to see what happened. They stood back, afraid. They gave her room, just in case the bully got up and started swinging. But instead he struggled to his feet and staggered off into the dark.

"Don't cry," Alma said to the Ninja Turtle. But tears were leaking from the boy's eyes. His bag had ripped, so the little kid crawled on his hands and knees, searching desperately for the candies that had spilled to the ground.

"Don't worry, we'll find them," Alma reassured him as she stooped to help him search.

"All my candies are gone," he wailed.

"You can have mine," she said. "Here."

She reached into her bag and brought out a full-sized Baby Ruth and a handful of other candies. Without hesitating, the Ninja Turtle snatched them and stuffed them greedily into his pockets.

After the fight Alma didn't feel like trick-or-treating. She walked up the street, cautiously looking around for the bully. She had surprised herself. She had acted on instinct, and her instinct now was to keep both eyes open and her fists doubled. She was afraid that he might be standing behind a tree with a stick. Or that maybe he had gone home to get his older brother. If only Manuel were still at home, Alma thought. She hid behind a tree when a car with only one headlight came up the street. As the car got closer, she could make out four teenagers. They were laughing and playing loud music.

After the car disappeared, after she had gathered enough strength, Alma ran to a house where the jack-o'-lantern out front had had its face kicked in.

"Trick or treat!" Alma yelled, trying to sound cheerful.

A woman came out, her face smeared with yellowish night cream. Spooked, Alma nearly jumped from fear at the sight of her.

"Lady——," Alma said, pointing at the jack-o'-lantern.

"This is the last straw," the woman growled, bending down to pick up the smashed pumpkin. "No more."

Alma left the woman to gather chunks of pumpkin and headed toward Sara's house two blocks away. She would surprise her friend, yell "Boo!" and then go home with her bag of treats. This is my last year, she reminded herself, hurrying now because there were fewer and fewer trick-or-treaters. It was getting late and cold. Some people were turning off their porch lights. The wind had picked up and was scattering the autumn leaves. In the distance a firecracker—or a gunshot—cut through the air. It made Alma jump and set her running. She became even more scared when a dog suddenly barked and leapt up at her from behind a fence.

"*¡Ay!*" she screamed. She ran even faster.

Alma was glad when Sara's house came into view. Lights were on in the house, and she could hear the thump of music.

"Trick or treat!" Alma yelled, rapping on the door. "Boo!" she screamed over the loud music. Alma wanted desperately to be let inside. She yelled again, "Boo, you stupid Sara. Let me in." But no one came to the door. Alma pounded on the door and rang the doorbell three times, but still no one answered. She decided to look through the front window. Cupping her hands around her eyes, she peered in. She realized, to her surprise, that Sara was giving a party. There were kids from school— Michael, Jesse, Julia, and Raul—dancing and laughing. There were pizza, sodas, and bowls of half-eaten ice cream.

"That darn Sara," Alma muttered, upset that she hadn't been invited.

Just then the front door opened and there stood Sara, a basket of candy in her hand. Sara, whose face was made up and who gave off the scent of sweet perfume, said, "I didn't hear you." She looked Alma up and down, adding as she held out the basket, "Gosh, you're tall."

"Trick or treat," Alma almost whispered, not knowing

what to do and wondering if she should run or hide her face. She took a Milky Way and a box of Nerds.

A boy from the party came to the door. It was Michael. "Who's that?"

"A trick-or-treater," Sara said. She thrust the basket of candy at Alma and said, "Here, have some more. We're turning off the porch light."

"He looks old enough to vote. You play for Roosevelt?"

"I'm a *she*, not a *he*, Michael," said Alma.

Sara and Michael looked bewilderedly at Alma. Michael peered under the helmet. "It's Alma," Michael said, laughing.

"Alma!" Sara said incredulously. She, too, peered beneath the helmet. "It is!"

They grabbed her jersey and pulled a reluctant Alma inside, yelling above the music, "Look, everybody! It's Alma Flores."

Someone turned down the music. Alma was embarrassed. Worse than that—she wished she could crawl under a rock and die. She took off her helmet, shaking out her long hair, which had become sweaty and tangled, and said, half smiling, "Trick or treat."

The crowd laughed and shouted back, "Trick or treat!" Alma smiled, feeling a bit better. Sara guided her to a table pushed to one corner of the living room and offered her a slice of pizza. The pizza was stiff and cold, but Alma was hungry for something salty and took a slice that was heavy with pepperoni and sausage.

"I'm sorry for not inviting you—," Sara started to say, but Alma cut her off. "Don't worry," she said, plucking a napkin from the table. "I was with some friends," she lied.

Alma had bitten into the pizza when she spotted the boy in the L.A. Raiders jacket who had tried to snag the Ninja Turtle's candy. The boy had just come out of the bathroom. He took a candy from his jacket pocket and offered it to a girl.

"My gosh," Alma said under her breath. She put her pizza down on the table.

The boy looked directly at Alma. For a second his eyes flashed with hatred. He muttered something, but Alma couldn't read his lips. The boy turned away and joined the crowd by the fireplace. The kids were warming themselves, their hands held out to the flames licking the logs red.

This is terrible, Alma thought, looking around the living room. None of them knew about this boy, certainly not Julia, who began to dance with him when the music was turned back up. The couple snapped their fingers and jerked their bodies about to the music. Alma noticed that although the boy was fat, his feet were tiny and rounded, like hooves. Her grandmother had warned her about people with small feet. The boy continued to dance, and with his narrow face he looked like a goat.

Alma squeezed shut her eyes and prayed that this was not happening. She prayed that she wasn't in Sara's house. When she opened her eyes, she could see flames from the fireplace flaring behind the dancers. The flames wagged like tongues over an ancient log.

"This is all wrong," Alma muttered. She looked around the living room. Everyone was dancing, and all their feet seemed small and pointy.

The boy stared at Alma and said something she couldn't hear. He smiled menacingly at her, a fang of light glinting in his mouth. For the first time in a long time, she remembered that Halloween was supposed to be scary, and that devils could appear even on a night when candies rained into paper bags all throughout a quiet town.

ƒIRST JOB

ON A HOT SUMMER DAY, Alex sat on the couch, sipping from a tall glass of homemade eggnog that he and his six-year-old brother, Jaime, had whipped up in the blender. They had followed a recipe from their mother's only cookbook. Alex had brought down a canister of sugar from the cupboard, and Jaime had carried the eggs and milk from the refrigerator. They'd washed their hands and begun to work. But immediately the sugar spilled.

"*Ay, menso*, look what you done!" Alex scolded. He scooped up a handful of sugar and tossed it back into the canister. He licked his palms for grains of sugar, one eye on Jaime.

Jaime followed suit. He ran his fingers over the spilled sugar and then licked them, from his little pinkie to his worm of a thumb.

"Come on, be careful," Alex said as he returned to

work. He measured the sugar and milk, and cracked an egg on the edge of the counter.

They managed to make the eggnog and were in a good mood as they sat in front of the TV, their glasses of eggnog less than half gone, watching a game show. The prize was a trip to Hawaii and the second prize was a refrigerator packed with eight different kinds of meat. The third prize was a set of encyclopedias, bound in imitation leather but stamped with real gold-leaf letters.

"I want to go to Hawaii before I die," Alex said, trying to start up a conversation.

"Does it snow there?" Jaime asked. A mustache of foam was stuck to his upper lip.

"No, man, that's where they got the ocean."

"I like snow better. But sometimes I like the ocean better because it's got sand."

"You don't know what you like." Alex stopped talking and turned his attention to the game show. My brother is hopeless, he thought.

It was Alex's job to watch his little brother while his parents and his older brother and sister worked. For the most part Alex didn't mind taking care of Jaime, but now and then when he saw what his brother and sister bought with the money they earned, he grew jealous and upset.

Why can't I get a *real* job? he asked himself when he saw his brother slip into a new shirt. Why?

First Patricia had gotten a job. She worked two days a week for Mrs. McIntyre, a nurse on the night shift at St. Agnes Hospital. Patricia did mostly housecleaning. She washed dishes. She shoved a rag behind lamps where dust gathered. She swept the floor and scoured the bathroom. She changed burned-out light bulbs. But she also washed the car, careful to work slowly because Mrs. McIntyre loved her Acura Legend more than anything in the world.

Then Alex's brother Bernardo, who was fourteen and only a year older than Alex, got a job with a gardener who cut lawns and hauled junk that was not really junk. They would turn around and sell this tossed stuff—lamps, chairs, racks of shoes, black-and-white TVs. Bernardo earned fifteen dollars a day, an eye-opening stash he kept in his sock drawer.

Today they were all at work. Alex was left alone with his little brother. His glass was now empty of eggnog, and he sighed from the heaviness of the midday drink. He touched his gut and burped.

"I'm bored," Alex said.

Jaime looked at his brother but didn't say anything. He was still loudly slurping his eggnog through a straw.

Alex went into the kitchen and saw the mess. The blender was sticky, the counter was sticky, and the eggshells were drooling idiotically.

"Aw, man," he said to himself. He tossed the eggshells into the trash and wiped the counter with a sponge. As he wiped the counter, he could hear the eggnog slosh in his stomach, moving back and forth like suds in a big washing machine. He burped again, the sweetness of eggnog filling his mouth.

Instead of returning to the living room to watch the rest 'of the game show, Alex went outside to the patio. Even though there was shade, the day was hot and flies flew lazy halos in the air. He picked up a tennis ball and began smacking it against the side of the house. He wanted to see if he could hit the ball thirteen times (his age and, for the time being, his lucky number) without missing. He did it once before he quit. It was too hot to play. Alex went out to the front yard and drank from the garden hose.

Across the street his neighbor Mrs. Martinez was sweeping leaves into a cardboard box. She was a neighbor who constantly played the small yellow radio that sat in her window. She was the one who knit a red woolly coat for her shivering Chihuahua named Princesa and warmed up her car for half an hour before backing out with both hands on the steering wheel. She was the neighbor who told on Alex when he and his friend Jésus tossed light bulbs in the alley.

"*Muchacho, ven acá,*" Mrs. Martinez yelled, waving at Alex. The flesh under her upper arm wiggled.

What does she want? Alex wondered, as he hiked up his pants and crossed the street.

"You rake and burn the leaves," she said in Spanish. She handed him a rake with three teeth missing that was held together with black electrical tape. "I will pay you a dollar."

"A dollar?" Alex asked. He thought of Bernardo, how at the end of the day he came home with fifteen dollars in cash. But then he thought that it wouldn't take long to rake the leaves. He should do it. It would be the start of his working career, and Mrs. Martinez was a sure-bet job reference.

Alex followed Mrs. Martinez to her backyard, where two large roosters the color of smoke clucked and pecked at the ground. Chickens looked up when Alex opened the gate and he and Mrs. Martinez entered.

Her yard was mostly taken up by fruit trees and a scraggly patch of chiles, squash, and tomatoes. A bed sheet hung on the line. A doghouse stood empty, a rusty chain attached to its side. A bathtub leaned against the shed, along with an assortment of wood that was so old that the paint had peeled.

Mrs. Martinez pointed to the tree. Even though it was summer, the tree, a bottle brush, was shedding leaves. "Rake and burn over there," she commanded. She pointed to a pile of junk along the back fence, then handed him three wooden matches from her apron.

Mrs. Martinez went inside, leaving Alex eyeing the chickens that were eyeing him. He stomped his foot and they jumped, sending a few feathers seesawing in the air.

Alex began raking, the leaves quickly gathering in the old rake. He found a quarter, caked with earth. He spat on it and cleaned the mud from President Washington's face. He saw that the coin had been minted in 1959.

"Man, it could be worth something," he said. He pocketed the quarter and resumed raking. While he worked he thought of his brother Bernardo, who was probably out somewhere running a lawn mower. His sister was probably wiping down Mrs. McIntyre's Acura Legend, the sunlight glinting off its perfect paint.

In no time Alex had raked the leaves and heaped them into a pyramid shape near the back fence. He wiped his sweaty face, then squatted down and struck a match against the wooden fence. The flame flared with a hiss and then calmed to a yellowish head of fire. He lowered the match into the leaves, which began to smoke and then caught fire.

Alex stood back, waving the smoke away from his face. He coughed and stared at the fire. He turned and saw that the chickens were pacing nervously near the gate.

"You scaredy-cats," he shouted. He struck one of the other matches and threw it in their direction, the match falling harmlessly nearby. He clapped loudly and the chickens jumped, their claws splayed in midair.

Then Alex remembered his little brother.

"*Ay,*" he said, his eyes growing big with worry as he hurried toward the gate. He would come back to collect his money as soon as he had checked on Jaime. He hoped Mrs. Martinez would pay him with a crisp dollar, not bitter pennies and grimy nickels. As he started to leave he plucked a tomato from her vine and bit into it. The tomato squirted seeds into his mouth.

Alex crossed the street and went inside his house. His brother was asleep on the couch, his empty glass of eggnog wedged between his legs. His upper lip was beaded with sweat, and his cheeks were pink. His curly hair looked soft. He looked like an angel, Alex had to admit. That's what their mother called Jaime—"angel" this, "angel" that.

"Wake up," Alex screamed. He turned off the television with a quick twist of his wrist. A man on the screen

was selling used cars and laughing when his face collapsed
into a shrinking gray dot and then vanished altogether.

"Come on, Jaime," Alex said. He shook his brother's
shoulders and pinched his cheek. Jaime's wobbly body
felt as loose and boneless as a Raggedy Andy doll.

Jaime woke slowly, rubbing his fists into his eyes. He
looked down at his empty glass, then gazed up at Alex
and asked, "Did you drink some of mine?"

"No, I was working." He held up the partially eaten
tomato. "Mrs. Martinez gave me a tomato."

Jaime, still sleepy, looked at his brother, trying to shift
his mind to wakefulness. "You were not," he said at last.

"I was. I was working for Mrs. Martinez. She's gonna
pay me a dollar." He pointed in the direction of Mrs.
Martinez's house.

Jaime got on his knees and looked outside. He didn't
have to rub his eyes to see smoke coming from Mrs.
Martinez's backyard.

"She's burning something," Jaime said. "Is she having
a barbecue?"

"What?" Alex asked.

Alex looked out the front window and saw a wafer
of smoke forming above Mrs. Martinez's roof. Her next-
door neighbor was hurrying toward her backyard, barefoot
and shirtless.

"Don't tell Dad," Alex begged, wagging a grimy finger
at his brother.

"Did you do something bad?" Jaime asked. "Dad said
if you do something wrong we can't go on vacation."

Without answering, without listening, Alex was out

the front door and flying across the street. Fear went up and down his back like a zipper. He could feel the lick of a belt across his legs, a fire that would die only when he held his legs under a cold, cold shower. He was in trouble, and he knew it.

"What have I done?" he muttered to himself. He threw the tomato into the gutter.

The neighbor stood, legs spread apart, squirting the small fire with a garden hose. The blaze had eaten the grass to a black stubble and had scared the chickens into the next yard. The smoky stench had pulled some kids from across the alley, and they had gathered to peek at the commotion.

"Turn on the water all the way," the neighbor said, motioning toward the faucet.

Alex did as he was told and stood motionless, paralyzed with fright.

When Alex realized the fire had climbed the fence and blackened some slats, he started to cry. His dime-sized tears fell to the ground. He coughed, and his nose began to run.

Mrs. Martinez rushed out onto the porch. She was carrying a telephone book in one hand and her dog in the other. Princesa's red coat was buttoned all the way up to her jingling dog tags.

Mrs. Martinez shouted, "Alex, I'm looking for the fireman. *¡Ayúdame!*"

"Mrs. Martinez, don't call," Alex begged tearfully. "I'll pay you." He stuck one hand into his pocket and fingered the third and last match, snapping it in two because he was so angry with himself. He thrust the hand back into his pocket and brought out the quarter he had stashed along with a handful of sunflower seeds. "Mrs. Martinez, this is worth money." He held up the quarter, and President Washington's face seemed to wink in the sunlight.

The neighbor, his eyes stinging from the smoke, turned and said, "It's almost out. It'll be OK."

Mrs. Martinez put down the book. She yelled at Alex, "*Mira*, you ruined my rake." She pointed at the rake leaning against the fence. It was charred, and now all its teeth were gone. "And my chickens are in Mrs. Silva's yard."

Alex looked toward Mrs. Silva's house. He could see one of the chickens perched in a tree, looking down at the Silvas' mean, snaggle-toothed cat, Gavacho. He wondered if his dad had meant what he'd said about not taking them on vacation.

Princesa barked at Alex, who gazed at his shoes in misery. He could hear the chickens in the next yard, clucking and scratching the hard-packed earth. And he could hear the kids asking what had happened.

So ended Alex's first summer job. Alex had hoped to earn a dollar, but it hadn't worked out that way. Instead his dad had to shell out ten dollars to replace some wood, and Alex had to help Mrs. Martinez rebuild her fence while Princesa yapped at his heels.

EL RADIO

AT 7:15 IN THE EVENING Patricia Ruiz's mother dabbed lipstick on her small, shapely mouth. Her father worked a red tie around his neck, swallowing twice so that his Adam's apple rode up and down. At 7:22 they were standing at the mirror in the bathroom, her mother rubbing Passion-scented lotion on her wrists and her father spraying Obsession in the cove of his neck.

They were in a rush to go to the opera, a recent interest Patricia couldn't understand. Only a year ago they'd spent every Friday night listening to the "Slow-Low Show" of oldies but goodies, hosted by "El Tigre." Now it was opera on Friday nights and a new Lexus in the driveway, a sleek machine that had replaced their '74 Monte Carlo.

"Lock all the doors, *mi'ja*," Patricia's mother said, swishing in her chiffon dress. Patricia's mother reminded her of a talking flower—she was slim as a stem and she gave off a bouquet of wonderful smells.

Her father came into the living room plucking lint from the sleeve of his jacket. Patricia thought her father was handsome: his trim mustache, the silver at his temples, his romantically sad-looking eyes. Her girlfriends said he resembled Richard Gere, especially when he wore a stylish suit, as he did now.

"Pat, I rented you a movie," her father said, pointing vaguely at the cassette on the coffee table. "We'll be home by ten-thirty, eleven at the latest."

From the couch, a *Seventeen* in her lap, Patricia watched her parents get ready for the evening. She thought they were cute, like a boyfriend and girlfriend brimming with puppy love.

"I'll be OK," she said. She got up from the couch and kissed them.

As her parents rushed out the front door, Patricia hurried to the telephone in the kitchen. Her best friend, Melinda, who lived two blocks away, was waiting for her call.

"They're gone," she announced. "Come on over."

Patricia hung up and took a can of frozen orange juice down from the freezer. Using one hand to spank the clods of frozen orange pulp with a paddlelike spoon until they broke apart, she snapped the fingers of her free hand and said, "It's party time!"

Patricia remembered that the "Slow-Low Show" of oldies but goodies was on the air. She turned on the small radio on the kitchen windowsill and the stereo in the living room. El Tigre, the host, was sending out the message: "Now this one goes out to 'Slinky' from 'Mystery Girl' in Tulare. And this goes to 'Johnny Y.' in Corcoran from 'La Baby Tears,' who says, 'I'll be waiting for you.' And we got special love coming from Yolanda to her old man, Raul, who says, 'Baby, I'm the real thing.' Yes, *gente*, the world turns with plenty of slow-low romance."

While El Tigre played "Let's Get It On," Patricia went back to the kitchen to make popcorn. She got a bottle of vegetable oil from the cupboard and a pot from the oven. The oven's door grated on her nerves when it squeaked open or closed. She was pouring corn kernels into the pot when Melinda pounded on the back door.

"Hey, *ruca*," Melinda said when Patricia unlatched the door. Melinda was a chubby classmate of Patricia's in eighth grade at Kings Canyon Junior High. She was wearing a short black dress, and her lipstick was brownish red against a pale face caked with makeup. Her eyelashes were dark and sticky with mascara.

"*Ruca*, yourself, *esa*," Patricia greeted her, shaking the pot over the burner and its flower of bluish flames. The kernels were exploding into white popcorn.

Melinda turned up the radio and screamed, "*Ay*, my favorite." "Ninety-Six Tears" was playing, and Melinda, standing at the counter, was pretending to play the keyboard. She lip-synched the words and bobbed her head to the beat. When the song ended, Melinda poured herself a glass of orange juice and asked her friend, "Patty, you ever count how many tears you cried?"

Patricia shook her head and started giggling.

"One time, when my mom wouldn't let me go to the Valentine's dance—the one last year when the homeboys from Sanger showed up—I cried exactly ninety-six tears," Melinda said. "Just like the song."

"Get serious," Patricia replied, her eyes glinting in disbelief. She poured the popcorn into a bowl and added just a pinch of salt because she'd heard a spoonful of salt was worse for your complexion than nine Milky Way candy bars devoured in an hour. "How can you count your tears?"

"I used my fingers."

"No way."

"De veras," Melinda argued. She rolled the fingers of one hand, her fingernails clicking against the counter.

The two girls took the popcorn and orange juice into the living room and cuddled up on the couch, careful not to spill. On the radio El Tigre was whispering, "This one goes out from Marta to 'El Güero.' And we got a late bulletin from Enrique to Patricia—"

"Hey, Patty, some guy's got eyes for you," Melinda said. Her eyes were shiny with excitement. She jumped up and boosted the volume of the stereo. "The message is," El Tigre continued, " 'don't get fooled by plastic love.' "

"I like that," Melinda said.

"Chale. No way," Patricia said, trying to laugh it off. She got up and turned down the volume. "I don't know no Enrique."

"Enrique de la Madrid!" Melinda screamed. "Danny's brother."

"That little squirt? The *vato* just lost his baby teeth last week."

The girls laughed and started dancing separately to Mary Wells's song, "My Guy." They continued dancing, fingers snapping and bodies waving in slow motion when the song segued into Marvin Gaye's "I Heard It Through the Grapevine."

When that song faded from a thumping bass to scratchy silence, Patricia and Melinda sat down on the couch, their legs folded beneath them. There was a glow of happiness about them, and their eyes were shiny. Patricia picked out a single popped kernel of corn and tossed it in Melinda's open mouth. Melinda threw a single popcorn at Patricia's mouth. It hit her in the eye, and they laughed and threw handfuls of popcorn at each other. They liked hanging out together. They could dance wildly and lip-synch nonsense lyrics without feeling stupid.

The two girls became quiet when El Tigre cleared his throat and whispered, "From Fowler, we celebrate the first but not the last anniversary of Susie and Manny. From us, *su familia*, steady love for that eternal couple. And check it out—real serious commotion from Softy, who says to his Lorena in Dinuba, 'Let's get back together.' "

When "Angel Baby" came on, the girls eased into the couch. They nursed their orange juices and slowly chewed their popcorn. They synched the words. Patricia figured that the singer's boyfriend must have found another girl, then lost that girl and joined the army.

Melinda looked at Patricia, who looked back at her. Melinda asked, "Anyone ever call you Angel Baby?"

Patricia sat up, giggling, and said, "*Cállate*, Melinda, you're ruinin' the song." But she thought briefly about Melinda's question. "No, no one's ever called me Angel Baby. But my dad calls me Sweetie."

"My dad calls me La Pumpkin."

"*Órale*. Your *papi's* got it right," Patricia laughed. She bounced off the couch and, heading to the kitchen, asked, "You want more orange juice?"

"*Simón, esa,*" Melinda said.

While Patricia was in the kitchen, Melinda gazed into the mirror on the far wall, where Patricia's baby pictures hung. She dabbed her lips with lipstick.

When Junior Walker and the All-Stars' "Shotgun" began its soulful blare, Melinda started chugging to the song, elbows churning at her side, singing, "You're a lousy, no-good, stinkin' Shotgun-n-n-n."

"Go, brown girl, go!" Patricia yelled when she returned. She put down the glasses of orange juice and chugged along with Melinda, elbows flapping at her sides like the wings of a chicken. They laughed and felt happy. When the song ended Patricia took a drink of orange juice.

"Yeah, we're gonna have to come up with a name for you, *ruca*," Melinda said. She sized Patricia up and, stroking her chin, said, "How 'bout La Flaca?"

"*Y tú*, La Pumpkin!" Patricia chided. She ran her hands down her hips. Yeah, I am skinny, she told herself, but at least I'm not a fat *mamacita!*

40

El Radio

"La Flaca!"

"La Pumpkin!"

"La Flaca!"

"La Pumpkin!"

The girls laughed at their nicknames and threw popcorn at each other. Then Melinda suggested that they call El Tigre to dedicate a song.

"*¿A quién?*" Patricia asked.

"Enrique de la Madrid," teased Melinda as she climbed over the couch and headed for the telephone in the hallway.

"*¡Chale!*" Patricia screamed, her heart pounding with fear and delight. "I don't like that squirt."

"But he's got eyes for you."

"You mean *you*."

"*Pues no.* You mean *you!*"

Patricia pulled on Melinda's arm, and Melinda pushed Patricia. Suddenly they were on the floor wrestling, each laughing and calling the other by her nickname. In the background El Tigre was whispering, "Now stay cool, *y* stay in school."

When Melinda reached for the telephone, the receiver fell off the hook and corkscrewed on its cord. Even though she had yet to dial the radio station, she was yelling, "*Esta ruca, se llama La Flaca de* Kings Canyon Junior High, wants to dedicate a song to her sleepy boyfriend. She wants—"

Patricia put her hand over Melinda's mouth and felt the smear of lipstick working into her palm. Melinda pulled Patricia's hair, lightly, and Patricia pulled on

Melinda, not so lightly. They struggled and laughed until Melinda said, "OK, OK, you win."

They both sat up, breathing hard but feeling good. After catching her breath, Patricia said, "I'll call El Tigre and have him do a *dedica* to my parents."

"¡Qué idea!"

Patricia dialed *El Radio*, and immediately she got El Tigre, who said in a low, low-riding voice, *"¿Qué pasa? Cómo te llamas, esa?"*

Without thinking, Patricia said, *"La Flaca y mi carnala La Pumpkin del barrio de* south Fresno."

"Y tu escuela?"

"Roosevelt High," Patricia lied. She didn't want El Tigre to know that he was rapping with a junior-high kid.

"And what oldy but goody do you want me to spin for you? *¿Y tu dedica?"*

"I wanna hear 'Oh, Donna,' by Ritchie Valens." Patricia moved the telephone to her other ear while she thought about the dedication. "And I . . . I want to dedicate the song to my parents, Jerry and Sylvia. I do love you, from your only but eternal daughter, Patricia."

"Pues, I'll get it on in a sec. Stay cool, *ruca,* and keep up the grades."

Patricia hung up, her heart pounding. She had never been so nervous. She put the telephone back on the table.

"You did good. 'Oh, Donna' is my next favorite," Melinda said. Melinda got up slowly from the floor and went to the mirror to tease her hair back into shape. She looked down at one hand and made a face. "*Ay*, Patty, you broke one of my fingernails."

Patricia felt her cheek. She was hot from wrestling and talking with El Tigre. The only other famous personality she had spoken to was Ronald McDonald when he had come down in a helicopter at the McDonald's on Kings Canyon Boulevard. And Ronald was nothing like El Tigre; he just gave away french fries, not oldies but goodies.

"You ever been on TV?" Patricia asked. She thought about her voice carrying over all of Fresno on the "Slow-Low Show."

"Nah," Melinda said. She had taken her compact out of her purse and was retouching her face. "I was in the newspaper once."

"You were?"

"Yeah, it was when they reopened the pool at Roosevelt. I was first in line." She closed the compact and brought out her mascara. "The paper was hard up for news."

The Supremes' "I Hear a Symphony" was playing on the radio, prompting Melinda to ask, "So your dad and mom are at the symphony?"

"Opera," Patricia corrected.

"They like that stuff?"

"*¿Quién sabe?* I think they want to try something they don't know about."

"Shoot, if I had their car I'd be cruisin' Blackstone," Melinda said. She began to fumble in her purse for her lipstick.

"But you don't have a license," Patricia said.

"*Pues*, I'll just put on some more makeup, and who can tell?"

At that moment the girls heard keys jingling at the front door. Melinda gave Patricia a frightened look. Patricia's eyes flashed, taking in the spilled popcorn, the blaring stereo, and the clock on the end table. It was only 9:35.

"It's either the cops or my parents," Patricia said.

"Same thing," Melinda said, rushing toward the kitchen in hopes of making it out the back door.

But it was too late. The door opened with a sigh, and the two girls found themselves staring at Patricia's shocked parents. Her father removed the key from the door, and her mother looked around the room trying to assess the damage.

"What's been going on?" her mother snapped as she walked toward Patricia. For a moment Patricia thought her mother was going to pinch her, but she only asked, "Are there any boys here?"

"No, just me and Melinda."

Her mother sniffed the air for boys and cigarettes. She saw the popcorn scattered over the rug.

"I spilled the bowl, Mrs. Ruiz," Melinda volunteered as she and Patricia scrambled to pick up the popcorn. "I tripped."

"I can't leave you alone! Can't I trust you?"

"Mom, we were just listening to El Tigre."

Patricia's father was quiet. He undid his tie and turned

down the stereo. He threw himself into his easy chair, feet up on the hassock.

"What's wrong?" Patricia asked her father. He seemed unusually quiet.

He turned his sad eyes to his daughter. "The car broke down."

"Broke down!" Patricia shouted.

"Yes, *broke down*," her mother repeated. Turning to Melinda, she asked, "Does your mother know where you are?"

"Ah, sort of," Melinda lied, her face turned away from Patricia's mother. She hated lying to grown-ups, especially parents with bad tempers.

Patricia's mother glared doubtfully at Melinda and muttered, "*Mentirosas*, both of you." She wiped away a few loose pieces of popcorn from the couch and sat down, her high heels dropping off her feet.

"You mean you didn't get to the opera?" Patricia asked. Before her mother or father could answer, the quick-thinking Melinda raced to the stereo and turned up the volume. El Tigre was whispering in his "Slow-Low," low-riding voice, "I'm coming at you at 9:39, and I hope you're kicking back in the heart of Aztlán."

"Yes, and I might be kicking these low-class *cholas* in the behind." Her mother spoke to the radio. Patricia could see that her mother was softening and that she and Melinda were out of danger.

"We got *una dedica*," El Tigre continued, "from Larry M. to 'Shy Girl' in west Fresno, who says, 'I lost a good thing.' To Gina of Los Banos, 'Happy Birthday,' from her father and mother. And from La Flaca to her parents, Jerry and Sylvia, 'I do love you, from your only but eternal daughter.' La Flaca has asked for 'Oh, Donna,' *y pues*, why not?"

"That's me, Mom. La Flaca!" Patricia yelled.

"You?" her mother asked, giving her daughter a questioning look.

"Yeah. I'm La Flaca and Melinda's La Pumpkin."

"My Dad calls me La Pumpkin," Melinda grinned.

Patricia's father laughed. He laughed long and hard until a single tear rolled from one of his eyes. "Did you hear these *cholas*? La Flaca *y* La Pumpkin." He got up and boosted the volume of the radio, which was playing "Oh, Donna." He asked his daughter playfully, "How'd you know my first girlfriend was named Donna?"

Patricia's mother slapped his arm and said, "*Ay, hombre.* Now look at you with a broken-down Lexus."

"Dad, you should have kept the Monte Carlo," Patricia said, feeling truly out of trouble.

"Yeah, you're right." He smiled wearily.

"Come on, Dad, let's dance," Patricia suggested.

"Let's party down!" Melinda yelled. She chugged off to the kitchen, lip-synching the words to "Oh, Donna."

"The heck with the opera," Patricia's father said after a moment of hesitation. "It's better with El Tigre." He took his daughter's hands in his and they danced, one-two, one-two, while Patricia's mother snapped her fingers to the beat. In the kitchen Melinda stood at the stove making a new batch of popcorn.

PUSH-UP

APRIL BROUGHT WIND, rain, blossoms, and for Carmen Durango, an orange-and-white kitten that she named Push-up. The cat was the color of ice cream on a stick—the kind you push up and lick until all that's left is a ring of cardboard and a sweetness dancing on your tongue.

Carmen found the kitten on the hood of her father's new used Chevy, a Caprice Classic with one bumper slapped on from some other car. He had bought the car from a young guy going into the service, and he had major plans for it—a new engine, a new paint job, a redyed vinyl roof.

"Oh, you're so cute," Carmen cooed. She had gone outside to get the Sunday newspaper for her father and found the kitten licking morning dew from the hood. The kitten looked up with dew on her whiskers. She meowed, took a few sprightly steps and slid off the hood, landing on her paws.

"Are you hurt?" Carmen asked as she rushed to the kitten. The kitten, purring, nudged against Carmen's "Hello Kitty" robe. Carmen picked up the kitten and hugged it. It was the prettiest thing she had ever seen.

"You look like an ice cream," Carmen said, rubbing her nose against the kitten's moist nose. "I'm going to name you Push-up. Do you like that name?" When the cat meowed, Carmen hugged it tightly. She hurried back inside with the newspaper in one hand and the kitten in the other.

That had been last Sunday. Her mother and father had said she could keep the kitten, even though they had an older cat named Tommy. When Tommy saw Push-up licking milk from his bowl, his face narrowed. Tommy hissed and started after Push-up, who raced away and hid under the refrigerator.

"Tommy, you bad, bad cat!" Carmen scolded. Tommy's face softened. Carmen picked up the older cat and, petting him, said, "She's your little sister. You can't hurt your little sister." She pressed her nose against Tommy's hot dry nose.

When she let him down, Tommy slinked to his bowl and drank all the milk, his back to the refrigerator where Push-up's front paws appeared first, then her head, then the rest of her tiny body. She seemed to have swallowed her meow, it was so faint. Carmen picked her up and cooed, "Oh, you poor baby."

It had been a trying Sunday for Carmen, and for Push-up. Tommy chased Push-up from one room to the next, from the kitchen to the living room to Carmen's bedroom. Carmen scolded Tommy, who would put his ears back and look sad for a moment. But once Carmen was out of view, helping her father with the yard or doing her homework, Tommy was after Push-up again.

That Sunday Push-up slept with Carmen, who liked the sound of her purring and the warmth of her furry but fragile body. The kitten liked pressing her nose to Carmen's nose. It was something like love between them.

But during the night, while they were sleeping, Tommy crept into Carmen's bedroom and jumped on the bed. Tommy hissed and uttered a deep, monstrous growl, and Carmen woke up screaming. Tommy raced from the bedroom, scared. Carmen got up and closed the door, muttering, "*Qué* bother."

On Monday, before she left for school, Carmen had stood at the front door and warned Tommy to leave Push-up alone.

"*Es tu hermanita,*" she said. "Be nice."

But when she came home, Carmen found Tommy sitting in front of the refrigerator, tail swishing against the floor like a wiper blade. Push-up was cornered and her meow was weak, as if she had fallen into a hole and was calling for help from way below.

Carmen, dropping her book bag, was shocked. "You meany," she yelled, grabbing Tommy by the scruff of his neck and pushing him away. Tommy sauntered slowly into the living room.

Tuesday morning Carmen again warned Tommy.

Lying by the floor furnace, the older cat had seemed more mellow and forgiving. He blinked his soft, lazy eyes at Carmen. Push-up, in turn, was beginning to adjust to her new surroundings. She ran after a rubber ball. She jumped for Carmen's sock. She leapt into the air when she heard Carmen's father scrape a chair against the floor.

But when Carmen returned home, she found Push-up in the breadbasket on top of the refrigerator, meowing for her life. Tommy was nowhere to be seen, but Carmen knew that he was involved; he'd probably chased the kitten all over the house for six hours straight. While Carmen had been doing math and English, Tommy had been smacking Push-up on the side of the head.

"Tommy!" she yelled. She rolled a newspaper and went looking for him. She found him in her parents' bedroom. He was looking out the window from a chair piled with magazines. He seemed distant and detached, so much so that Carmen petted and soothed him. She scratched behind his ears and pressed her cool nose to his dry, hot one. "I know it's difficult for you. But you're still our favorite," Carmen lied. "Push-up is just a baby."

Instead of growing bigger and healthier as a baby would, Push-up seemed to have shrunk. The kitten seemed nervous and exhausted. Now when she meowed, only air came out; she sputtered like an inner tube going flat. Carmen was concerned. She placed Push-up on the bathroom scale: the kitten weighed less than two pounds. She placed Tommy on the scale and was amazed to discover that he weighed twelve pounds. It was like comparing a feather to a sack of potatoes.

"*Mi'ja*, maybe you should make a bed for Push-up outside," Carmen's mother suggested Wednesday evening just before dinner. "You know we have to keep Tommy inside."

Tommy had been declawed. If he were let outside, he would have no way to protect himself. Mrs. Silva's cat, Bongo, would tear him apart. That cat was rumored to have killed and eaten a grown chicken, bones and all, even the few feathers that the wind didn't pick up and scatter.

"Mom, it's too sad. Push-up is just a kitten," she said. At that moment she heard the thump of paws against the carpet and raced into the living room. Tommy had cornered Push-up, and his face was a hatchet of hate.

"Bad cat!" Carmen scolded.

On Thursday Carmen decided to take Push-up to school. She knew there were rules against bringing animals to school, but she thought Push-up would die if she didn't get at least one day of rest from Tommy.

After her mother and father left for work, Carmen emptied her book bag and placed Push-up inside, along with a sandwich bag filled with cat crunchies. Push-up jumped out, scared. Carmen caught her and placed her back inside the bag. The second time was more difficult because Push-up's claws were out and she clung to the cloth bag.

When Carmen closed the front door on Tommy and his hostile antics, Push-up seemed more scared than when she was being chased by the cat. She meowed loudly from inside the swinging book bag.

"Don't cry," Carmen said in a soothing voice. Carmen walked hurriedly up the street. Every now and then she looked into the book bag. The kitten seemed worried and lost.

Carmen walked the three blocks to her school, John Burroughs Elementary, where she was a fifth-grader. She was sort of popular and had been chosen to be secretary of her class. She became nervous when she entered the school grounds. She walked around a knot of boys shoving one another. She looked for her best friend, Cecilia, and found her at the tetherball, playing a game with a boy.

"Cecilia," she whispered, through cupped hands. Push-up peeked out from the bag and looked around. When she meowed, Carmen pushed her head back into the bag.

Seeing her friend, Cecilia left the game. Her opponent called her a cheating quitter, but she ignored the insult. The two girls hurried away and sat on a bench across the school grounds. Carmen had told Cecilia the night before she would be bringing her new kitten to school. Cecilia was excited and scared for her friend. She didn't want Carmen to get in trouble.

Carmen opened her book bag and out popped Push-up. The kitten stretched, yawned, and then jumped in the air.

"Oh, he's so cute," Cecilia said. "He's just like a Push-up!"

"It's a 'she,' " Carmen corrected. She grabbed the kitten and placed her in Cecilia's lap. Her friend looked around to see if the kids could see them, but they were too far away.

Carmen bent down to run a finger over the grass at her feet, swiping up the morning dew. She poked the damp finger at Push-up, but the kitten didn't lap up the moisture. Carmen opened the sandwich bag of cat crunchies and shook a few into her palm. She tried to make Push-up eat from her palm, but she wasn't hungry. The kitten only yawned, showing the girls the back of her grayish throat.

"What if you get caught?" Cecilia asked, pushing her long hair behind her ears.

"I don't know." Carmen had a distant look on her face. She worried that if her teacher found out about the cat, she would tell her parents. Her parents would probably make her give Push-up away. She imagined Push-up cuddled in the arms of another girl, and she felt jealous.

The school bell rang. The girls walked slowly toward the school buildings, but as they got close to their classroom, Cecilia ran ahead, leaving Carmen and Push-up behind.

"I thought she was my friend," Carmen snarled. She peered into the book bag. The kitten looked drowsy. "You're my true friend."

Right then an idea came to Carmen, and she stopped in her tracks. She decided to hide the kitten in the wooden box where the four-square and soccer balls were kept. No one will know, she thought to herself. She raced to the box behind the backstop. She opened the lid, brushing away a sticky spiderweb.

"It's for your own good," Carmen said as she took the drowsy Push-up from the book bag and lowered her between two deflated four-square balls. She poured a pile of cat crunchies at her paws. "I'll be back at recess."

Carmen hurried to class, barely getting to her seat before second bell. She was hot and breathing hard. She looked over at Cecilia, who was sharpening a pencil, her back straight and proper. Cecilia wouldn't look in her direction. She was playing stuck-up, Carmen decided. She didn't want to get involved.

"What a friend," she muttered. She made a face at Cecilia and opened a drawer in her desk to search for a pencil.

That period they did math and geography. Carmen had to lie to the teacher; she said she'd left her books at a cousin's house, where she had spent the night because her parents were out of town. Because Carmen was a good student, the teacher didn't scold or punish her. She let her borrow a book that belonged to a boy who was absent.

When the bell rang for recess, Carmen flew out of the classroom, her skirt lifting high and her ponytails whipping her shoulders. She tore open the lid of the box. Push-up was pawing one of the balls.

"Oh, you're so cute," Carmen said, bending over to gather Push-up into her arms. The kitten blinked from the sunlight, and Carmen could see she was chewing on something. "What are you eating?"

Carmen pried open the kitten's mouth and, pushing

her finger in, brought out the chomped remains of what looked like a grasshopper. "*Asco*, you dirty little thing."

Disgusted, Carmen placed Push-up into her book bag and walked briskly across the school yard, away from the racket stirred up by the kids who had started playing dodgeball and four-square.

Carmen lifted Push-up from the book bag and placed her on the grass, which was now dry from the soft, even warmth of the April sun. Push-up sniffed the grass and leapt straight up for no apparent reason. The kitten pranced and jumped and hissed.

"You're so funny," Carmen said, a smile cutting across her face. But the smile disappeared when she saw Cecilia coming toward them. "What does she want?"

Cecilia arrived sucking on a green Jolly Rancher candy. She asked, "How is Push-up?"

"What do you care?"

"Don't be mad at me, Carmen. If I get in trouble, my mom gets really mad."

"But I thought you were my friend."

"I am your friend. It's just that I can't get in trouble."

Carmen didn't say anything. She watched in silence as Push-up pranced and rolled in the grass. When the recess bell sounded, Carmen put Push-up back into the book bag and the three of them returned to the classroom.

"You'll see that I'm your friend," Cecilia said, hurrying away. Carmen looked around and realized that most of the kids were already in the classroom. She raced back outside to the box, lifted Push-up from the book bag, and placed her in her hiding place. Push-up sniffed a ball and pounced on it, her legs spread as if she were hugging it.

When Carmen returned to the classroom she saw that she had someone's homework on her desk. She looked closely at the paper and realized that it was Cecilia's. Cecilia had erased her own name and put Carmen's at the top of the page.

Cecilia looked over at Carmen, who blew her friend a kiss. Cecilia would get marked down for not doing her homework, all because she was a true friend.

While the class studied art and spelling, Carmen began to worry about Push-up. She worried that maybe there was not enough air in the box and so her kitten would suffocate. After all, the box was a tight little space and now the sun was heating up the day. Carmen imagined Push-up meowing for air and gasping for a drink of water. Carmen breathed deeply—as if sucking air for her dying cat—and raised her hand.

The teacher walked up the aisle and asked, "What is it, Carmen?"

Carmen raised one finger and the teacher nodded, knowing what she meant.

But instead of going to the rest room, Carmen raced to the box and threw open the lid. Push-up was on her back, cleaning herself.

"Oh, you're alive," Carmen gasped. She petted the cat, and Push-up snapped playfully at her finger.

Carmen propped a rock between the lid and frame of the box to make sure Push-up would have fresh air.

She returned to class to take a spelling test. At the sound of the lunch bell, Carmen raced, with Cecilia in tow, to the box. When she opened the lid, she was shocked to discover the kitten was gone.

"Cecilia, what am I going to do?" Carmen cried.

Cecilia took out all of the balls and searched. The cat was gone, but as they both started to cry, they heard a faint meow.

"Push-up!" Carmen said.

"Where is she?" Cecilia asked, scanning the school grounds.

"I hope no one stole her," Carmen said.

"No, she ran away. We'll find her," Cecilia said in a reassuring voice.

They quietly began their search but stopped when they heard the kitten meow again. They ran to the fence that circled the school. Push-up was in a yard across the street.

"Oh, no," Carmen whined, stomping her foot.

"She's a little pest," Cecilia said.

A truck passed, its engine roaring. For a moment the girls thought that Push-up would run into the street and get smashed flat as a baseball glove. Carmen hid her face in her hands, too afraid to look.

But the truck passed, and Push-up rolled onto her back, pawing playfully at a leaf.

Abandoning all caution, Cecilia, who was a strong athlete, pulled herself over the fence and crossed the street to retrieve Push-up. The kitten bit her wrist and pawed at her ponytails.

Cecilia returned to the school grounds and handed Push-up to Carmen, who scolded her cat, "You naughty thing." She hugged her friend, whispering into her neck, "You're the best."

Racing from the box to the classroom, then racing from the classroom to the box—that's how it went all day, until the final bell. Carmen and Cecilia were sickened when they opened the box and discovered Push-up batting a small gray mouse that was playing dead.

"Push-up!" the girls screamed. They yanked the kitten from the box and, turning the box over and scattering the balls, let the mouse go free. The mouse lay still for a moment, then opened its eyes. It looked around, its whiskers quivering, and then ran away.

"Qué cochina," Carmen hollered. "How could you? A sweet mouse like that."

Push-up licked her paws, claws splayed, and then pawed at Carmen's wagging finger.

School was over, but not Carmen's ordeal. On the walk home Push-up leapt from the book bag, climbed into a tree, and refused to come down. It wasn't until a high school student walked by and climbed the tree that the kitten was retrieved.

When Carmen finally arrived at home she was in a huff about her orange-and-white kitten. She unlocked the front door and roughly plopped Push-up on the couch. Tommy, who was snuggled in her father's chair, stared hard at Push-up, his face once again a mask of hatred. He stood up, arching his back and hissing. He leapt toward the kitten, and the race was on—from one corner of the living room to the next. Carmen threw herself on the couch, deaf to Push-up's faint, desperate meows.

"Get her," Carmen snarled. Push-up had her back arched, fur sticking straight up. "Hit her one, Tommy."

Tommy jabbed a paw at Push-up, and Push-up rolled onto her back, paws thumping and a weak growl rising from her throat.

Carmen went to the kitchen for a snack. She returned to the living room with a glass of orange juice and a bag of sunflower seeds. Tommy now had Push-up cornered under the television. Carmen flicked on the TV with the remote control, scaring the two cats. Push-up bumped her head against the bottom of the television.

Tommy raced after Push-up, and the kitten squealed from terror as she bounded for safety in Carmen's lap. Push-up raised her sad eyes to her owner. She tried to press her nose to Carmen's.

"Oh, so you want me now, huh?" Carmen cooed with a smile on her face, pressing Push-up's nose like a button. "You want me to protect you, huh? Fat chance!"

Carmen set Push-up on the floor and lightly spanked her tail. She turned up the volume of the television. She didn't want to hear Push-up's cries as Tommy raced after her throughout the house, on an afternoon in April when the spring winds were blowing blossoms from the trees.

THE SCHOOL PLAY

IN THE SCHOOL PLAY at the end of his sixth-grade year, all Robert Suarez had to remember to say was, "Nothing's wrong, I can see," to a pioneer woman who was really Belinda Lopez. Belinda was one of the toughest girls since the beginning of the world. She was known to slap boys and grind their faces into the grass until they bit into chunks of wormy earth. More than once Robert had witnessed Belinda staring down the janitor's pit bull, a dog that licked his frothing chops but didn't dare mess with her.

The class rehearsed the play for three weeks, at first without costumes. Early one morning Mrs. Bunnin wobbled into the classroom carrying a large cardboard box. She wiped her brow and said, "Thanks for the help, Robert."

Robert was at his desk etching a ballpoint tattoo—

D-U-D-E—on the mountaintops of his knuckles. He looked up and stared at his teacher. "Oh, did you need some help?" he asked.

She rolled her eyes at him and told him to stop writing on his skin. "You'll look like a criminal," she scolded.

Robert stuffed his hands into his pockets as he rose from his seat. "What's in the box?" he asked.

She popped open the Scotch-taped top and brought out skirts, hats, snowshoes, scarves, and vests. She tossed Robert a red beard, which he held up to his face thinking it made him look handsome.

"I like it," Robert said. He sneezed and ran one hand across his moist nose.

His classmates looked at Robert in awe. "That's *bad*," Alfredo said. "What do I get?"

Mrs. Bunnin threw him a wrinkled shirt. Alfredo raised it to his chest and said, "My dad could wear this. Can I give it to him after the play is done?"

Mrs. Bunnin turned away in silence.

Most of the actors didn't have speaking parts. They were given cut-out crepe-paper snowflakes to pin to their shirts or crepe-paper leaves to wear.

During the blizzard scene in which Robert delivered his line, Belinda asked, "Is there something wrong with your eyes?" Robert looked at the "audience," which for rehearsal was all the things that filled the classroom: empty chairs, a dented world globe that had been dropped by almost everyone, one limp flag, one wastebasket, and a picture of George Washington, whose eyes seemed to follow you around the room when you got up to sharpen your pencil. Robert answered, "Nothing's wrong. I can see."

Mrs. Bunnin, biting on the end of her pencil, said, "Louder, both of you."

Belinda stepped forward, her nostrils flaring so that the shadows on her nose quivered, and said louder, "Sucka, is there something wrong with your eyeballs?"

"Nothing's wrong. I can see."

"Louder! Make sure the audience can hear you," Mrs. Bunnin directed. She tapped her pencil hard against the desk. "Robert, I'm not going to tell you again to quit fooling with the beard."

"It's itchy."

"We can't do anything about that. Actors need props. You're an actor. Now try again."

Robert and Belinda stood center stage as they waited for Mrs. Bunnin to call "Action!" When she did Belinda approached Robert slowly. "Sucka face, is there anything wrong with your mug?" Belinda asked. Her eyes were flecked with anger. For a moment Robert saw his head grinding into the playground grass.

"Nothing's wrong. I can see."

Robert giggled behind his red beard. Belinda popped her gum and smirked. She stood with her hands on her hips.

"What? What did you say?" Mrs. Bunnin asked, pulling off her glasses. "Are you chewing gum, Belinda?"

"No, Mrs. Bunnin," Belinda lied. "I just forgot my lines."

The play, *The Last Stand*, was about the Donner party,

with the action taking place just before the starving members of the expedition started eating each other. Everyone
who scored twelve or more out of fifteen on the spelling
tests got to say at least one line. Everyone else had to
stand around and be trees or snowflakes.

Mrs. Bunnin wanted the play to be a success. She
couldn't risk having kids with bad memories on stage.
The nonspeaking trees and snowflakes hummed to create
the effects of snow flurries and blistering wind. They
produced hail by clacking their teeth.

Robert's mother was proud of him because he was
living up to the legend of Robert DeNiro, for whom he
was named. During dinner he said, "Nothing's wrong. I
can see," when his brother asked him to pass the dish
towel, their communal napkin. His sister said, "It's your
turn to do dishes," and he said, "Nothing's wrong. I can
see." His dog, Queenie, begged him for more than water
and a Milkbone. He touched his dog's own hairy beard
and said, "Nothing's wrong. I can see."

One warm spring night Robert lay in the backyard
counting shooting stars. He was up to three when David,
a friend who was really more his brother's friend, hopped
the fence and asked, "What's the matter with you?"

"Nothing's wrong. I can see," Robert answered. He
sat up, feeling good because the line came naturally, without much thought. He leaned back on his elbow and asked
David what he wanted to be when he grew up.

"I don't know yet," David said, plucking at the grass.
"Maybe a fighter pilot. What do you want to be?"

"I want to guard the president. I could wrestle the

assassins and be on television. But I'd pin those dudes, and people would say, 'That's him, our hero.' " David plucked at a blade of grass and frowned.

Robert thought of telling David that he really wanted to be someone with a super-great memory who could recall facts that most people thought were unimportant. He didn't know if there was such a job, but he thought it would be great to sit at home by the telephone waiting for scientists to call him and ask hard questions.

The three weeks of rehearsal passed quickly. The day before the play, Robert felt happy as he walked home from school with no homework. As he turned onto his street, he found a dollar floating over the currents of wind.

"A buck," he screamed to himself. He snapped it up and looked for others. But he didn't find any more. It was his lucky day, though. At recess he had hit a fluke home run on a bunt—a fluke because the catcher had kicked the ball, another player had thrown it into center field, and the pitcher wasn't looking when Robert slowed down at third, then burst home with dust flying behind him.

That night was his sister's turn to do the dishes. They had eaten enchiladas with "the works," so she slaved away in suds up to her elbows. Robert bathed in Mr. Bubble, the suds peaked high like the Donner Pass. He thought about how full he was and how those poor people had had nothing to eat but snow. I can live on nothing, he thought, and whistled like wind through a mountain pass, flattening the Mr. Bubble suds with his palm.

The next day after lunch he was ready for the play, red beard in hand, his one line trembling on his lips. Classes were herded into the auditorium. As the actors dressed and argued about stepping on each other's feet, Robert stood near a cardboard barrel full of toys, whispering over and over to himself: "Nothing's wrong. I can see." He was hot, itchy, and confused. When he tied on the beard, he sneezed. He said louder: "Nothing's wrong. I can see," but the words seemed to get caught in the beard. "Nothing, no, no. I can see great," he said louder, then under his breath because the words seemed wrong. "Nothing's wrong, can't you see?" "Nothing's wrong. I can see you." Worried, he approached Belinda and asked if she remembered his line. Balling her hand into a fist, Belinda warned, "Sucka, I'm gonna bury your ugly face in the ground if you mess up."

"I won't," Robert said as he walked away. He bit a fingernail and looked into the barrel of toys. A clown's mask stared back at him. He prayed that his line would come back to him. He would hate to disappoint his teacher and didn't like the thought of his face being rubbed into spiky grass.

The curtain parted slightly and the principal stepped out, smiling, onto the stage. She said some words about pioneer history and then, stern-faced, warned the people in the audience not to scrape their chairs on the freshly waxed floor. The principal then introduced Mrs. Bunnin, who told the audience about how they had rehearsed for weeks.

Meanwhile the class stood quietly in place behind the

curtain. They were ready. Belinda had swallowed her gum because she knew this was for real. The snowflakes clumped together and began howling.

Robert retied his beard. Belinda, smoothing her skirt, looked at him and said, "If you know what's good for you, you better do it right." Robert felt nervous when the curtain parted, and his classmates—the snow, wind, and hail—broke into song.

Alfonso stepped forward with his narrative about a blot on American history that would live on forever. He looked at the audience, lost for a minute. But he continued, saying that if the Donner party could come back, hungry from not eating for over a hundred years, they would be sorry for what they had done.

The play began with some boys in snowshoes shuffling around the stage, muttering that the blizzard would cut them off from civilization. They looked up, held out their hands, and said in unison, "Snow." One stepped center stage and said, "I wish I had never left the prairie." Another said, "California is just over there." He pointed, and some of the first-graders looked in the direction of the piano.

"What are we going to do?" one kid asked, pretending to brush snow off his vest.

"I'm getting pretty hungry," another said, rubbing her stomach.

The audience seemed to be following the play. A ribbon of sweat ran down Robert's face. When it was time for his scene he staggered to center stage and dropped to the floor, just as Mrs. Bunnin had directed, just as he had seen Robert DeNiro do in that movie about a boxer. Belinda, bending over him with an "Oh, my," yanked him up so hard that something clicked in his elbow. She boomed: "Is there anything wrong with your eyes?"

Robert rubbed his elbow, then his eyes, and said, "I can see nothing wrong. Wrong is nothing, I can see."

"How are we going to get through?" Belinda boomed, wringing her hands together in front of her schoolmates in the audience, some of whom had their mouths taped shut because they were known talkers. "My husband needs a doctor." The drama advanced through snow, wind, and hail that sounded like chattering teeth.

Belinda turned to Robert and muttered, "You mess-up. You're gonna hate life."

But Robert thought he'd done OK. At least, he reasoned to himself, I got the words right. Just not in the right order.

After finishing his scene he joined the snowflakes and trees, chattering his teeth the loudest. He bayed like a hound to suggest the howling wind and snapped his fingers furiously in a snow flurry. He trembled from the cold.

The play ended with Alfonso saying again that if they were to come back to life, the members of the Donner party would be sorry for having eaten each other. "It's just not right," he argued. "You gotta suck it up in bad times."

Robert remembered how one day his sister had locked him in the closet and he didn't eat or drink for five hours.

When he got out, he hit his sister, but not so hard it left a bruise. Then he ate three sandwiches and felt a whole lot better. Robert figured that Alfonso was right.

The cast paraded up the aisle through the audience. Belinda pinched Robert hard, but only once because she was thinking that it could have been worse. As he passed a smiling and relieved Mrs. Bunnin, she patted Robert's shoulder and said, "Almost perfect."

Robert was happy. He'd made it through without passing out from fear. Now the first- and second-graders were looking at him and clapping. He was sure everyone wondered who the actor was behind that smooth voice and red, red beard.

THE RAIDERS JACKET

LORENA ROCHA PARTED the curtain in her living room and looked out onto the wet street. The rain was still coming down but with less windblown fury. A shaft of sunlight even appeared, poking through the elm tree at the curb. Lorena smiled and then stopped. The sunlight faltered and disappeared as a cloud once again blocked the sun.

Earlier that Saturday morning it had been coming down, as her father said at breakfast, *"como gatos y perros."* If it didn't stop raining soon it would ruin her day. She wanted her mother to drive her to the mall at Fashion Fair, but her mother didn't like to drive in rain—and for a good reason: driving in the rain, she had once gotten into an accident that ripped a mailbox from its cemented bolts.

Lorena and her best friend since first grade, Guada-

lupe, were desperate to go to the mall. They had to replace
a Raiders jacket.

The Wednesday before, Eddie Contreras, the hand-
somest seventh-grader in their class (if not all of Fresno,
California), had given Lorena his jacket to wear.

She had been after Eddie relentlessly since September,
and in the second week of October, during lunch, he
finally took off his jacket and draped it over Lorena's
shoulders. She smiled like a queen. She could feel the
warmth of his body in the jacket. Her cheeks blossomed
into twin roses of happiness.

"OK, but I want it back tomorrow," he said, walking
away with his friend, Frankie Medina, who looked back,
winked, and gave Lorena the thumbs-up sign.

"Qué guapo," Guadalupe had said. "I think he likes
you."

"Do you think so?" Lorena asked, twirling so that the
jacket flared. The sleeves were long and hid her hands.
And the collar was as itchy as her father's face at the end
of a workday. Still, it was hers for one day. She pushed
her hands into the pockets and found a piece of chewing
gum, which she tore in half and shared with Guadalupe.
It was Juicy Fruit, their favorite.

The two of them were happy and walked around the
school yard, parading for all their friends. One girl snapped
the gum in her mouth and asked point-blank, "You and
Eddie tight?" Lorena didn't answer. Embarrassed, she hid
her face behind the sleeves of Eddie's jacket.

When the bell rang Lorena and Guadalupe separated.

Lorena went to French class, where she sat warm as a bird in the nest of Eddie's jacket. She went dreamy with deep longing. She kept picturing herself and Eddie running in slow motion down a windswept beach, each of them wearing a Raiders jacket, each of them draped in silver and black. Her smiling face was soft, with a faraway look. When the teacher called on her to conjugate the verb "to swim" in French, Lorena, still lost in her dream, said, *"Nado, nadas, nada, nadamos, nadan"*—the Spanish, not the French, conjugation.

During her last class, biology, Lorena overheard a group of whispering girls. One said, "Eddie and Lorena . . . I think they're stuck on each other."

If only it were true, Lorena thought. She hugged herself and felt the warmth of the jacket. For a moment, the beach scene replayed itself in the back of her mind.

The biology teacher made them cut apart dead frogs. He had been telling them for weeks that they would be dissecting a frog and that they should get used to the idea. He had said that dissecting a frog was no different than cutting apart a barbecued chicken.

"Gross," several of the students said, twisting their faces into ugly knots of disgust.

It *was* gross, Lorena thought. She took the knife in her hand and pierced the skin with a quick jab. She was surprised the frog didn't jump up, open its eyes, look at her, and plead, "Cut it out!"

She removed Eddie's jacket because she didn't want to get blood or gook on it. She folded it and placed it on a chair. Then she returned to dissecting, her face souring when the frog's slit belly opened, revealing a tangle of intestines.

When the bell rang Lorena tossed her half-skinned frog back into a white pan and hurried out of the class. She always had to hurry because the bus she caught for home left promptly ten minutes after school let out. She had to hurry more than usual that day because she had to stop in the office to pick up a release. Her French teacher was taking them to see a movie the next week.

She picked up the form, then raced to board the bus that stood idling in front of the school. The driver was reading a newspaper. His coffee was up on the dash, growing cold.

Lorena waved out the window to Guadalupe, who rode another bus. "I'll call you when I get home," she yelled at her friend, who was pushing a boy who was trying to make her smell his froggy hands.

Lorena found a seat. After a few minutes the driver folded his newspaper, drank his coffee in three gulps, wiped his mouth on his sleeve, and muttered, "Hang on."

The bus lurched and was coughing a black plume of smoke when Lorena looked out the window and saw Eddie and his friend, Frankie, stomping on milk cartons. An explosion of milk burst into the air, scaring two girls who were standing nearby.

Lorena's hands went straight to her shoulders. "The jacket!" she screamed. She shot from her seat and ran up the aisle to the driver.

"You've got to stop! I forgot Eddie's jacket!"

"Who's Eddie? I don't know no Eddie," the driver said, shifting into third. "Sit down."

"I lost his jacket!" she screamed, stomping her foot like a little girl.

The driver downshifted as he came to a red light. He turned to her, his lined face dark with stubble. He warned her again with a wag of one ink-stained finger, "I said, sit down."

And she did. She returned to her seat and sat clutching her books. "How can I ever tell Eddie?" she whimpered. She closed her eyes and pictured herself telling him. He was standing by his locker, trying to remember his combination. He wore a T-shirt, the braille of goose bumps on his arms. Outside it was raining hard.

That was Wednesday afternoon. Lorena was frantic that evening when she spoke in hushed tones to Guadalupe on the telephone in the hallway at home.

"How could I be such a *mensa?*" she scolded herself as she sat cross-legged, the telephone cradled in one hand and a cookie in the other. She blamed her biology teacher for her problem. If he hadn't made them dissect frogs, she wouldn't have been so absentminded.

The next day Lorena rushed from the bus to the biology room. The jacket was not there.

"Darn it," she snarled, pounding her fist on a table. She turned angrily and shot a fiery glance at the frogs that had been tossed into the white pan to await first period.

She decided to keep her distance from Eddie by sneaking down the hallways pretending to be reading a book.

She spent most of her break and lunch period in the rest room, brushing her hair and worrying. Now and then Guadalupe would come into the rest room to tell her where Eddie was and what he was doing. He had been slap-boxing with Frankie.

Lorena and Guadalupe decided to stay home Friday so that Lorena could avoid Eddie. She spent the day reading *Seventeen* and eating bowls of saltless popcorn.

The girls decided that they would pool their money and go shopping on Saturday to replace the jacket. Lorena figured she had about eighty dollars, and with Guadalupe's thirty-four dollars, her life savings, they would have enough to buy a new Raiders jacket.

It had been rainy when Lorena awoke Saturday morning, and Guadalupe was really sick but still willing to go with her to Fashion Fair.

"Mom," Lorena called as she walked into the kitchen. "It's stopped raining."

"Did you clean your room?" her mother asked. She was sitting at the kitchen table cutting coupons from the *Fresno Bee* newspaper.

"Two times. I even cleaned the aquarium."

Her mother sighed as she stood. Peeking out the kitchen window, she saw that the rain had let up. It was still misty, but the skinny plum tree they had planted last winter was no longer wavering in the wind. Her mother said, "OK, but you don't have to get me anything fancy."

Lorena had told her mother she wanted to go shopping so that she could buy her a gift for her birthday, which was the next week.

They drove to pick up Guadalupe, who climbed into the car and immediately sneezed. She had a wad of
crumpled Kleenex in her fist.

"*Ay*, I bet you got a cold from going outside with
your hair wet," Lorena's mother said, accelerating slowly.
She didn't want to chance running into a mailbox again.

"I caught a cold from my stupid brother," Guadalupe
said. She turned to Lorena and, leaning into her shoulder,
whispered, "I got ten more dollars."

They drove in silence to Fashion Fair.

"I don't want you two to fool around," Lorena's
mother warned as she let the girls out. She tried to look
serious, but both of them knew that she was a softy.

Lorena promised to behave. Guadalupe sneezed and
said, "Thank you, Mrs. Rocha. I'll be sure that Lorena
doesn't act up."

Lorena pushed Guadalupe, who laughed and said,
"Well, I *am* older."

"But not wiser, *esa*."

The two girls watched the car pull away with Mrs.
Rocha gripping the steering wheel with both hands. Then
they walked into the mall and headed toward Macy's,
which was at the other end. Guadalupe wanted to stop
and buy an Orange Julius drink, but Lorena hissed, "Lupe,
we may not have enough money!"

"Yeah, you're right," Guadalupe said, stopping to open
her purse. She rifled through it—eyeliner, an old report
card, gum, sticky Lifesavers, a scrap of paper with the
phone number of a so-so-looking boy from Tulare. Her
fingers at last squeezed the envelope that contained forty-

four dollars. She looked around before handing the envelope to Lorena. "You can pay me back in a month, right?"

"I think I can," Lorena said, her eyes big with excitement. The envelope weighed a lot, and Lorena slipped it into her coat pocket. "Lupe, you're a real friend."

The girls hurried to Macy's, and Lorena thrust her hand into her pocket every now and then to be sure the envelope was still there. They rode the escalator to the second floor and headed for the men's department, where two salesmen were standing near the cash register. They were bent over with laughter, apparently cracking up from a joke. Except for three other shoppers, the department was empty. It was quiet, too, except for the thump of music from an overhead speaker.

Lorena wanted to go unnoticed. She didn't want the salesmen to help. She and Guadalupe slid past them without being seen and stopped at a rack of Raiders jackets.

"I don't know what size Eddie wears," Lorena said, placing one hand to her chin as she studied the jackets. She took one from the rack and tried it on. The sleeves came down over her hands. "This looks like the size."

"Are you sure?" Guadalupe asked.

"No," she said after a moment. She slipped out of the jacket and looked at the tag inside—size 36. "Guadalupe, try it on."

"Me?" Guadalupe said, pointing a finger tipped with a polished nail at herself.

Guadalupe was an inch taller and twenty pounds heavier than Lorena, a *gordita* to a *flaca*. She slipped the jacket on, arms outstretched, and asked, "How does it look?"

Lorena squinted and remarked, "I don't know. But I think it's the same size as Eddie's." She scanned the other jackets on the rack. She had to be sure.

"Why don't you just tell Eddie the truth?" Guadalupe suggested. "Then he can get his own jacket."

"I'm gonna look like a fool," Lorena said. "I don't want him to know I lost his jacket." She clicked a fingernail against her front teeth and stared at the rack. She stared some more and then replaced the jacket. "I think it was a size 34."

She walked to the cash register with the size 34 jacket. The salesmen were no longer laughing. One was helping a woman who was complaining about a broken zipper, and the other was punching a number into the telephone. When the second salesman saw Lorena, he hung up and asked, "Will this be all?"

"Yeah," she said, her hands shaking. Lorena brought out the envelope and the money from her own purse.

The salesman smiled and said, "Nice jacket. For your boyfriend?" He wagged his head from side to side and smiled, showing his clean, white teeth.

Lorena paid and took the shopping bag from the salesman. "Let's get outta here," she whispered. The two girls rode the escalator down a level and headed for the perfume department, where they dabbed their wrists with the richness of love and passion.

"My mom would like this," Lorena said of a perfume emblazoned with Liz Taylor's signature. "Too bad I don't have enough money."

Neither of the girls was in a good mood. Neither of them liked spending all their money, especially Lorena. She had been saving her money to buy a moped when she turned sixteen and could get her license. Now that dream—*and* the dream of running in slow motion on the beach with Eddie—was dead.

Lorena and Guadalupe left Macy's and were standing in front of Hickory Farms inhaling the smells of 63 different cheeses and meats when they heard Eddie's voice. They turned and saw Eddie and his friend Frankie, both of whom were devouring bags of popcorn.

"Hey, Lorena, how come you left my jacket in biology?" Eddie asked coolly after he cleared his throat of popcorn. "I thought you liked me."

Lorena nearly fainted. This wasn't a dream. It was a nightmare—in silver and black. Eddie was wearing his Raiders jacket and a sneer on his face.

"Eddie, your jacket," Lorena blurted. She reached out to touch it, but Eddie pulled away. He took a step back and then said to Frankie, "The janitor found my jacket."

"I can explain," Lorena pleaded. "I didn't want to get any frog on your jacket—" Lorena stopped in midsentence. The story sounded ridiculous.

All the while Guadalupe stood staring at her shoes. She saw that her white laces had turned gray and wet from the rain. Her eyes filled with tears for her friend.

"Just leave me alone, *esa*," Eddie said.

Frankie licked his lips and said, "How could you do this to *mi carnal?* Man, he was treating you nice, *loca*."

After Eddie and Frankie left, chewing their popcorn

casually as camels, Lorena and Guadalupe found a quiet place for a good cry. Lorena's tears fell, as her father would say, *como gatos y perros.*

"Eddie will never like me," she sobbed.

"There are bigger fish," Guadalupe comforted her.

They cried into each other's coats, then wiped their eyes and dabbed the buds of their mouths with lipstick. They returned the jacket and bought Lorena's mother some meats and cheeses, not the romantic perfumes called Passion or Ecstasy that filled their noses when they thought of love.

THE CHALLENGE

FOR THREE WEEKS José tried to get the attention of Estela, the new girl at his middle school. She's cute, he said to himself when he first saw her in the cafeteria, unloading her lunch of two sandwiches, potato chips, a piece of cake wrapped in waxed paper, and boxed juice from a brown paper bag. "Man, can she grub!"

On the way home from school he walked through the alleys of his town, Fresno, kicking cans. He was lost in a dream, trying to figure out a way to make Estela notice him. He thought of tripping in front of her while she was leaving her math class, but he had already tried that with a girl in sixth grade. All he did was rip his pants and bruise his knee, which kept him from playing in the championship soccer game. And that girl had just stepped over him as he lay on the ground, the shame of rejection reddening his face.

He thought of going up to Estela and saying, in his best James Bond voice, "Camacho. José Camacho, at your service." He imagined she would say, "Right-o," and together they would go off and talk in code.

He even tried doing his homework. Estela was in his history class, and so he knew she was as bright as a cop's flashlight shining in your face. While they were studying Egypt, José amazed the teacher, Mrs. Flores, when he scored twenty out of twenty on a quiz—and then eighteen out of twenty when she retested him the same day because she thought that he had cheated.

"Mrs. Flores, I studied hard—*¡de veras!* You can call my mom," he argued, his feelings hurt. And he *had* studied, so much that his mother had asked, "*¿Qué pasó?* What's wrong?"

"I'm going to start studying," he'd answered.

His mother bought him a lamp because she didn't want him to strain his eyes. She even fixed him hot chocolate and watched her son learn about the Egyptian god Osiris, about papyrus and mummification. The mummies had scared her so much that she had heated up a second cup of chocolate to soothe herself.

But when the quizzes had been returned and José bragged, "Another A-plus," Estela didn't turn her head and ask, "Who's that brilliant boy?" She just stuffed her quiz into her backpack and left the classroom, leaving José behind to retake the test.

One weekend he had wiped out while riding his bike, popping up over curbs with his eyes closed. He somersaulted over his handlebars and saw a flash of shooting stars as he felt the slap of his skin against the asphalt. Blood rushed from his nostrils like twin rivers. He bicycled home, his blood-darkened shirt pressed to his nose. When he examined his face in the mirror, he saw that he had a scrape on his chin, and he liked that. He thought Estela might pity him. In history class she would cry, "Oh, what happened?" and then he would talk nonsense about a fight with three *vatos*.

But Estela had been absent the Monday and Tuesday after his mishap. By the time she returned on Wednesday his chin had nearly healed.

José figured out another way to get to know her. He had noticed the grimy, sweat-blackened handle of a racket poking out of her backpack. He snapped his fingers and said to himself, "Racquetball. I'll challenge her to a game."

He approached her during lunch. She was reading from her science book and biting into her second sandwich, which was thick with slabs of meat, cheese, and a blood-red tomato. "Hi," José said, sitting across the table from her. "How do you like our school?"

Estela swallowed, cleared her throat, drank from her milk carton until it collapsed, and said, "It's OK. But the hot water doesn't work in the girls' showers."

"It doesn't work in ours either," he remarked. Trying to push the conversation along, he continued, "Where are you from?"

"San Diego," she said. She took another monstrous bite of her sandwich, which amazed José and made him think of his father, a carpenter, who could eat more than anyone José knew.

José, eager to connect, took a deep breath and said, "I see that you play racquetball. You wanna play a game?"

"Are you good?" Estela asked flatly. She picked up a slice of tomato that had slid out of her sandwich.

"Pretty good," he said without thinking as he slipped into a lie. "I won a couple of tournaments."

He watched as the tomato slice slithered down Estela's throat. She wiped her mouth and said, "Sure. How about after school on Friday."

"That's tomorrow," José said.

"That's right. Today's Thursday and tomorrow's Friday." She flattened the empty milk carton with her fist, slapped her science book closed, and hurled the carton and her balled-up lunch bag at the plastic-lined garbage can. "What's your name?"

"Camacho. José Camacho."

"I'm Estela. My friends call me Stinger."

"Stinger?"

"Yeah, Stinger. I'll meet you at the courts at 3:45." She got up and headed toward the library.

After school José pedaled his bike over to his uncle Freddie's house. His uncle was sixteen, only three years older than José. It made José feel awkward when someone, usually a girl, asked, "Who's that hunk?" and he would have to answer, "My uncle."

"Freddie," José yelled, skidding to a stop in the driveway.

Freddie was in the garage lifting weights. He was dressed in sweats and a Raiders sweatshirt, the hem of his T-shirt sticking out in a fringe. He bench-pressed 180 pounds, then put the weights down and said, "Hey, dude."

"Freddie, I need to borrow your racquetball racket," José said.

Freddie rubbed his sweaty face on the sleeve of his sweatshirt. "I didn't know you played."

"I don't. I got a game tomorrow."

"But you don't know how to play."

José had been worrying about this on his bike ride over. He had told Estela that he had won tournaments.

"I'll learn," José said.

"In one day? Get serious."

"It's against a girl."

"So. She'll probably whip you twenty-one to *nada*."

"No way."

But José's mind twisted with worry. What if she did, he asked himself. What if she whipped him through and through. He recalled her crushing the milk carton with one blow of her fist. He recalled the sandwiches she downed at lunch. Still, he had never encountered a girl who was better than he was at sports, except for Dolores Ramirez, who could hit homers with the best of them.

Uncle Freddie pulled his racket from the garage wall. Then he explained to José how to grip the racket. He told him that the game was like handball, that the play was off the front, the ceiling, and the side walls. "Whatever you do, don't look behind you. The ball comes back—fast. You can get your *ojos* knocked out."

"Yeah, I got it," José said vaguely, feeling the weight of the racket in his hand. He liked how it felt when he pounded the sweet spot of the strings against his palm.

Freddie resumed lifting weights, and José biked home, swinging the racket as he rode.

That night after dinner José went outside and asked his father, "Dad, has a girl ever beaten you at anything?"

His father was watering the grass, his shirt off and a stub of cigarette dangling from his mouth. His pale belly hung over his belt, just slightly, like a deflated ball.

"Only talking," he said. "They can outtalk a man any day of the week."

"No, in sports."

His father thought for a while and then said, "No, I don't think so."

His father's tone of voice didn't encourage José. So he took the racket and a tennis ball and began to practice against the side of the garage. The ball raced away like a rat. He retrieved it and tried again. Every time, he hit it either too softly or too hard, and he couldn't get the rhythm of a rally going.

"It's hard," he said to himself. But then he remembered that he was playing with a tennis ball, not a racquetball. He assumed that he would play better with a real ball.

The next day school was as dull as usual. He took a test in history and returned to his regular score of twelve out of twenty. Mrs. Flores was satisfied.

"I'll see you later," Estela said, hoisting her backpack onto one shoulder, the history quiz crumpled in her fist.

"OK, Estela," he said.

"Stinger," she corrected.

"Yeah, Stinger. 3:45."

José was beginning to wonder whether he really liked her. Now she seemed abrupt, not cute. She was starting to look like Dolores "Hit 'n' Spit" Ramirez—tough.

After school José walked slowly to the outdoor three-walled courts. They were empty, except for a gang of sparrows pecking at an old hamburger wrapper.

José practiced hitting the tennis ball against the wall. It was too confusing. The ball would hit the front wall, then ricochet off the side wall. He spent most of his time running after the ball or cursing himself for bragging that he had won tournaments.

Estela arrived, greeting José with a jerk of her chin and a "Hey, dude." She was dressed in white sweats. A pair of protective goggles dangled around her neck like a necklace, and she wore sweatbands on both wrists. She opened a can of balls and rolled one out into her palm, squeezing it so tightly that her forearm rippled with muscle. When she smacked the ball against the wall so hard that the echo hurt his ears, José realized that he was in trouble. He felt limp as a dead fish.

Estela hit the ball repeatedly. When she noticed that José was just standing there, his racket in one hand and a dog-slobbered tennis ball in the other, she asked, "Aren't you going to practice?"

"I forgot my balls at home," he said.

"Help yourself." She pointed with the racket toward the can.

José took a ball, squeezed it, and bounced it once. He was determined to give Estela a show. He bounced it again, swung with all his might, and hit it out of the court.

"Oops," he said. "I'll go get it, Stinger."

He found the ball in the gutter, splotched with mud that he wiped off on his pants. When he returned to the court Estela had peeled off her sweats and was working a pair of knee pads up her legs. José noticed that her legs were bigger than his, and they quivered like the flanks of a thoroughbred horse.

"You ready?" she asked, adjusting her goggles over her eyes. "I have to leave at five."

"Almost," he said. He took off his shirt, then put it back on when he realized how skinny his chest was. "Yeah, I'm ready. You go first."

Estela, sizing him up, said, "No, you go first."

José decided to accept the offer. He figured he needed all the help he could get. He bounced the ball and served it into the ground twice.

"You're out," she said, scooping the ball up onto her racket and walking briskly to the service box. José wanted to ask why, but he kept quiet. After all, he thought, I am the winner of several tournaments.

"Zero-zero," Estela said, then served the ball, which ricocheted off the front and side walls. José swung wildly and missed by at least a foot. Then he ran after the ball, which had rolled out of the court onto the grass. He returned it to Estela and said, "Nice, Estela."

"Stinger."

"Yeah, Stinger."

Estela called out, "One-nothing." She wound up again and sizzled the ball right at José's feet. He swung and hit his kneecap with the racket. The pain jolted him like a shock of electricity as he went down, holding his knee and grimacing. Estela chased the ball for him.

"Can you play?" she asked.

He nodded as he rose to his feet.

"Two-nothing," she said, again bouncing the ball off the front wall, this time slower so that José swung before the ball reached his racket. He swung again, the racket spinning like a whirlwind. The ball sailed slowly past him, and he had to chase it down again.

"I guess that's three to nothing, right?" José said lamely.

"Right." Estela lobbed the ball. As it came down, José swung hard. His racket slipped from his fingers and flew out of the court.

"Oops," he said. The racket was caught on the top of the chain-link fence surrounding the courts. For a moment José thought of pulling the racket down and running home. But he had to stick it out. Anyway, he thought, my backpack is at the court.

"Four-nothing," Estela called when she saw José running back to the court, his chest heaving. She served again, and José, closing his eyes, connected. The ball hit the wall, and for three seconds they had a rally going. But then Estela moved in and killed the ball with a low corner shot.

"Five-nothing," she said. "It's getting cold. Let me get my sweats back on."

She slipped into her sweats and threw off her sweat-bands. José thought about asking to borrow the sweat-bands because he had worked up a lather of sweat. But his pride kept him quiet.

Estela served again and again until the score was seventeen to nothing and José was ragged from running. He wished the game would end. He wished he would score just one point. He took off his shirt and said, "Hey, you're pretty good."

Estela served again, gently this time, and José managed to return the ball to the front wall. Estela didn't go after it, even though she was just a couple of feet from the ball. "Nice corner shot," she lied. "Your serve."

José served the ball and, hunching over with his racket poised, took crab steps to the left, waiting for the ball to bounce off the front wall. Instead he heard a thunderous smack and felt himself leap like a trout. The ball had hit him in the back, and it stung viciously. He ran off the court and threw himself on the grass, grimacing from the pain. It took him two minutes to recover, time enough for Estela to take a healthy swig from the bottle of Gatorade in her sport bag. Finally, through his teeth, he muttered, "Good shot, Stinger."

"Sorry," Estela said. "You moved into my lane. Serve again."

José served and then cowered out of the way, his racket held to his face for protection. She fired the ball back, clean and low, and once again she was standing at the service line calling, "Service."

Uncle Freddie was right. He had lost twenty-one to

nada. After a bone-jarring handshake and a pat on his aching back from Estela, he hobbled to his uncle's house, feeling miserable. Only three weeks ago he'd been hoping that Estela—Stinger—might like him. Now he hoped she would stay away from him.

Uncle Freddie was in the garage lifting weights. Without greeting him, José hung the racket back on the wall. Uncle Freddie lowered the weights, sat up, and asked, "So how did it go?"

José didn't feel like lying. He lifted his T-shirt and showed his uncle the big red mark the ball had raised on his back. "She's bad."

"It could have been your face," Freddie said as he wiped away sweat and lay back down on his bench. "Too bad."

José sat on a pile of bundled newspapers, hands in his lap. When his uncle finished his "reps," José got up slowly and peeled the weights down to sixty pounds. It was his turn to lift. He needed strength to mend his broken heart and for the slight chance that Stinger might come back, looking for another victory.

ᴨACHO LOCO

ONE MORNING Ignacio "Nacho" Carrillo's fifth-grade teacher, Mrs. Wigert, brought the book *Fifty Simple Things Kids Can Do to Save the Earth* in to class. She talked about recycling cans and bottles, repairing leaky faucets, planting trees, doing away with Styrofoam, and snipping six-pack rings so birds wouldn't get their necks caught.

"Earth, after all, is our mother," Mrs. Wigert said, and one of the bad boys in the back rows replied, "Yo momma!"

Mrs. Wigert shushed the boy, a finger to her lips. She scanned the class, asking for quiet. Then she announced, "I'm a vegetarian. Do you know what a vegetarian is?"

"It's when you don't like meat," said Desi, a fat boy whose *chones* could be seen when he ran.

"It's when you just eat grass," Leticia said.

"Not grass, Leticia—noodles," Robert corrected.

Mrs. Wigert smiled at these definitions. She said, "It's when you decide not to eat meat for the welfare of your body and the planet."

"I ain't on welfare!" Robert snickered.

The class laughed, and Mrs. Wigert frowned. She clapped the book closed and said that they would go on to math. As she stood up behind her desk, her stomach rumbled, making her sound very, very hungry.

But Nacho had listened to what she said. He knew what a vegetarian was because his brother, Felipe, had gone to college and come back with ideas that would solve the world's problems. His brother had decided not to buy anything at department stores and dressed in clothes from the Salvation Army thrift store on Tulare Street.

"You're supposed to be educated," his father grumbled at his oldest son. "*¿Por qué te vistes en garras?* Why are you dressed in rags?"

"*Mi'jo,* what will your *abuelita* think?" his mother pleaded.

His father and mother had worked hard to send their son to college, and now, to their minds, he looked like a bum.

And Felipe was a vegetarian.

Yes, Nacho knew what a vegetarian was, and at that moment, as he opened his math book and licked his pencil preparing to do division, he decided to become one. Mrs. Wigert was right, he thought. We must save the planet in small ways.

Nacho left the classroom a committed vegetarian—

or at least determined to become one after he ate his lunch, which was weighed down with a thick bologna sandwich. He liked bologna, especially when his mom also packed corn chips in his lunch. He would open his sandwich and methodically place nine corn chips to form a square, as if he were playing tick-tack-toe. Then he'd put it together, close his eyes, and take a big bite, the corn chips crunching in his ears.

And that's what his mother had packed in a paper bag today: a bologna sandwich and corn chips, along with a box of juice and a plastic bag of carrot sticks. Nacho looked at the carrot sticks and put them aside. Then he went to town on the sandwich.

Nacho ate with his friend, Juan, on a bench outside the cafeteria. Juan was one of the best baseball players at school and he could shoot hoop, fight, and keep up with the smartest girls in a spelling bee. He was everything Nacho was not. Nacho was a dreamer, quick to pick up on the most recent scientific fad. Once he read in the "Grab Bag" section of the newspaper that if you place a dull razor blade under a pyramid structure and point it south, the pyramid's energy will restore the sharpness of the blade. He tried it with his father's old blades and wrapped them up as a Christmas present. Unfortunately, the blades remained dull, and his poor father had ended up with nicks from his throat to his upper lip.

"I'm not eating meat after this," Nacho said. "It's bad for the world."

"What are you talking about?" Juan said. His cheeks were fat with bites from a tuna sandwich.

"I'm a vegetarian."

"A what?"

"A vegetarian. I'm a person who thinks of mankind. I won't eat meat anymore." Nacho bit into his juicy bologna sandwich, savoring the taste, eyes closed.

"But you're eating meat now, ain't you?" Juan asked.

"This is the last time," Nacho said, wiping his mouth on the paper bag. His mother had forgotten to pack him a napkin.

"That's weird," Juan said. "Won't you get sick if you don't eat meat?"

"Mrs. Wigert is a vegetarian," Nacho commented.

"She's already grown," Juan said. "Anyways, I like hamburgers."

Nacho saw in his mind's eye a hamburger wrapped in a greasy wrapper and finger-sized french fries steaming on a white plate. He shook the images off and eyed his carrot sticks. He took one out from the sandwich bag and held it in his lips like a cigarette.

"And I don't smoke either," he said, laughing.

After lunch they played baseball, but their game ended when Juan hit the ball onto the roof of a building. Nacho had batted only once, hitting a feeble grounder back to the pitcher.

After school Nacho and Juan walked home together. Both of them were hungry so they stopped at the corner grocery store. Juan scraped up enough money in the corners of his pockets to buy a Hostess cupcake. Nacho bought a package of beef jerky, using the money he got from recycling aluminum cans on Saturday.

"I thought you were a vegetarian," Juan said as they left the store. He tore off the Hostess cupcake wrapper and threw it absentmindedly on the ground.

Nacho's mouth fell open in shock. He stopped in his tracks and confessed, "I am, but I forgot." He looked at the beef jerky; the little chunks reminded him of scabs. But since he had already paid for the beef jerky, he reasoned that it was worse to throw away food than to eat it. He was sure vegetarians would never throw anything away. They would always eat everything on their plates or, in this case, in their packages.

Juan's cellophane scuttled in a light breeze, and Nacho picked it up.

"I'll trade you then," Juan said.

Nacho bit his lip because at the moment he preferred salt to sugar. Reluctantly he handed over his beef jerky. He took Juan's cupcake and stuffed it in his mouth; its chewy sweetness dissolved in three bites. For the rest of the walk home he had to watch Juan tear off pieces of jerky and chew slowly, the smoky juice dripping from his mouth.

Nacho's mother was in the kitchen when he arrived home. The radio was tuned in to Mexican news—a bus had gone off a cliff in Monterrey.

"Hi, Mom," he greeted her, throwing his books on the kitchen table.

"How was your day, *mi hombrecito?*" she asked. She

looked up from whacking a round steak with her favorite black-handled kitchen knife. Nacho looked at the round steak, then at the puddle of blood leaking from the meat, and announced, "Mom, I'm a vegetarian."

"*¿Qué?*" she asked. She turned over the steak and started pounding the other side.

"I'm a vegetarian. I don't eat meat anymore."

His mother stopped pounding the steak and wiped her brow with the back of her hand. "Son, don't tell me you're like Felipe."

"Mom, meat is bad for you."

"Meat is good for you. It'll make you *más fuerte.*" She made a muscle in her right upper arm.

"Scientists have done studies, Mom. They say our teeth are supposed to eat only vegetables."

"*Ay, Dios,* where did we go wrong!" she cried, her chopping hand waving the kitchen knife.

"Mom, it's for the welfare of our bodies and mankind."

"*Estás chiflado,* just like your brother," she groaned. "And you didn't even go to college." She pounded the steak furiously and mumbled under her breath that when she had been a girl in Mexico, she'd been lucky to eat meat. At the start of a lecture about the old days in Michoacán, when his mother had been the daughter of a poor florist and weekend harpist who plucked his life away at a restaurant, Nacho tiptoed out of the kitchen. He went to his bedroom, which he shared with his little brother, Isaac.

Isaac was watching TV on a small black-and-white set they'd gotten from an uncle who'd needed ten bucks for gas.

"TV's bad for you," Nacho said.

Isaac took his eyes off the television for a second and said, "So?"

"I'm just saying, it's bad. Go ahead and do what you want. I'm a vegetarian." But the television caught Nacho's attention. There was a Burger King commercial of a guy jamming a double patty into a hungry grin. Nacho's mouth began to water.

He went outside and played slapball against the garage door. But each time he missed, or the ball ricocheted away from him, he would run past an old cardboard pizza box that had been left on the redwood table under the patio. Nacho remembered that pizza. His father had been promoted to foreman at Valley Irrigation. He and Nacho's mother had gone out to celebrate with their *compa* and brought back spicy pepperoni pizza for the kids.

Nacho played slapball until his father came home, and then the two of them shot hoop. They played a quick game to twelve, one point per basket. His father was big around the middle but a sweet outside shooter.

"You're just a little *piojo*, but you'll grow," his father said, wiping his face with the sleeve of his work shirt. He sat on the back steps. His chest was heaving, and the lines on his throat glistened with sweat.

"Dad," Nacho said, "I think I might be a vegetarian."

"*Qué dices?*" his father asked, his face still.

"Today we had a talk about the world. Mrs. Wigert said eating meat is bad for you."

"So?"

"So, I'm a vegetarian. I don't eat meat anymore."

"*¿Qué hacen a mi familia?* First your brother and now you?" His father got up and turned on the garden hose. He drank long and hard from it. He patted his belly and then agreed, "OK, you be a vegetaran . . ."

"*Vegetarian*," Nacho said.

"Yes, but you'll be such a *flaco* we won't know where you are," he said playfully. "Not like this." He smacked his belly and laughed.

His father went inside, leaving Nacho on the back steps staring at the empty pizza box. When he finally went inside, his older brother, Felipe, was in the kitchen, lowering a piece of *carne asada*—marinated round steak—into his mouth.

"Hey, Felipe," Nacho said, his stomach suddenly grumbling from emptiness.

"Hey, you little Nacho-head," Felipe said to his brother. "Give me five."

They slapped each other's hands. Then Nacho said, "I thought you were a vegetarian."

"Not anymore. My girlfriend left me."

"What?"

"Yeah, she moved on to greener pastures. A lawyer. I guess she doesn't like accountants."

"You mean you were a vegetarian because of your girlfriend?" Nacho was shocked. He turned on the faucet in the kitchen and washed his hands.

"Sort of. But I have a new girlfriend. She likes good food and bad movies."

"But I thought you had principles!"

"I do. But I got a new girlfriend."

Nacho felt cheated. He wanted to tell Felipe that he had become a vegetarian, but he kept quiet.

From the dining room their father called, "*Hombres, let's eat.*"

"Chow time," Felipe said.

Felipe sat down, a napkin crushed in one hand and a fork shining in the other. After a prayer of thanks, during which he kept his eyes open looking at the meat, Felipe dove into the *carne asada*. He ate like a barbarian, ripping a tortilla and pinching up smudges of *frijoles*.

"See, if you were living at home you would be eating good," his mother said as she passed him another tortilla from the basket.

"*Claro,*" he said.

Nacho sat in front of his plate of rice and beans. He took a forkful of beans, eyeing his brother's plate, which was loaded with steaming meat. He looked at his little brother's face, his mother's face, and his father's dark and stubbled face: they were all enjoying meat. They were barbarian meat-eaters.

Later Nacho helped do the dishes. He rinsed while his mother washed, and he kept turning around and looking at the stove; the pan of meat still rested on one of the burners. His mouth watered.

After the dishes were done, the family sat and watched a sitcom on television. Nacho didn't care about the program, except when one of the actors lifted a fork or wiped his mouth on a cloth napkin. But he zeroed in on the Denny's commercial and its parade of fried chicken, burgers, club sandwiches, bacon and eggs, and milk shakes. While they watched television, Nacho's father told his son Felipe that he was proud of him.

"You went all the way," he said. "In a few years it will be Nacho's turn. Already he has big ideas, like being a . . . *cómo?*"

"A vegetarian," Nacho's mother said. She had changed the channel to *las noticias*, the evening news.

"Yes, a human who doesn't eat meat," his father said. "How he will grow, *no sé.*"

"That's cool," Felipe said to Nacho. "Start young. What grade are you in?"

"Fifth," Nacho said, staring at a commercial for Pioneer Chicken.

"Yeah, go to State. I'll tell you about financial aid."

"Yes, ask about money. This ol' burro won't last," his father said, pointing to himself and braying like a donkey. "Ask your teacher *también.*"

Nacho heard some of their chatter, but his eyes were locked on the screen. A bucket of chicken was being devoured by a family of five, just like their family. Nacho's mouth flooded with the waters of hunger, and he had to leave the living room to eat a cracker.

Nacho went to bed hungry but determined not to ruin the planet. He lay awake, thinking about food, and when he closed his eyes, he saw a floating chicken drumstick.

But as he moved toward sleep he told himself that he should get serious. The next day he was going to ask Mrs. Wigert about college—financial aid, majors, and easy courses. And in privacy, away from Juan and the others, he was going to ask point-blank: how can you live without meat?

THE SQUIRRELS

ELIZABETH AGUIRRE AND HER five-year-old brother, Leonard, sat on the curb, a plastic bag at their feet. They had been walking door-to-door selling boxes of peanut brittle and mints, and coloring books of superheroes no one had ever heard of.

"Who's Man of the Universe?" one snide fat boy asked, his mouth red from Kool-Aid.

"Who's Iron Fist?" another snide but skinny boy asked.

Elizabeth and Leonard had no answers. They were trying to sell a hundred dollars' worth of candy and coloring books. In return they would get ten dollars plus a coloring book. They were tired and hot. And they were hungry. They thought of ripping open one of the boxes, but they knew they would have to account for it.

"We only sold three boxes," Elizabeth said, discouraged.

Leonard didn't say anything. He stomped on a line of red ants and stood, swatting more ants from his pants.

Elizabeth rose, too. She shook the hem of her dress and said, "Let's go."

They wandered up the street, Elizabeth swinging the plastic bag on her arm and Leonard dragging a stick. The sun baked the street, and the faint breeze stayed in the sycamores lining the curbs. The children stopped at a house where a man in a baseball cap was watering his lawn. His shirt was off, and a tattoo of a panther stood on his large belly, growling. Elizabeth was sickened by this sight, but she approached the man, reciting a formula sales pitch, "Good afternoon, sir. We're offering a line of delicious peanut brittle and mints at introductory prices."

"Huh?" the man responded.

"We're offering peanut brittle and mints . . ."

"Huh?" He moved his hose to a new patch of dry, scraggly lawn.

"We got peanut brittle and mints. They're real good."

The man threw down his garden hose, turned off the water, and hiking up his pants, approached the two children, who took a step back. Close up, his tattooed belly was scary.

"Are you selling Christmas cards? Ain't you early for Christmas?" he asked. "Let me see."

"Sir, we're selling candy," Elizabeth answered, trying not to look at his tattoo. "And coloring books."

Elizabeth took out the candy, and Leonard held the bag, smiling toothlessly. He had already lost his front teeth.

The man took the boxes, rattled their contents, and turned them over. "They seem old," he said after studying the list of ingredients.

"No, they're right from the factory," Elizabeth countered. "We just got them yesterday."

"How much?" the man asked, handing the boxes back to Leonard.

"Four dollars."

"Four dollars!" the man nearly hollered.

"This candy is straight from the factory—honest. The mints have one hundred percent natural flavorings and the peanuts are from Georgia." Elizabeth had been instructed to say this when customers balked at the price.

"Plus," she added, "it gives us a summer job. We're staying out of trouble and off the streets."

Leonard held up four sticky fingers and mumbled, "Sir, it's four dollars."

The man turned away and said, "Oh, no, not for me. I can get that at Safeway for half the price. These candies are soft." The children saw a tattoo of a growling bear clinging to his back. They left and crossed the street.

"That man should put a shirt on. He's creepy," Elizabeth whispered to Leonard, who had picked up another stick and was dragging it. They walked toward a small, tidy house with a green, green lawn trimmed with bright yellow flowers.

"Put that stick down," Elizabeth told her brother. He

threw it in the gutter and wiped his hands on his pants. "Remember to smile."

"OK," he said. A smile lifted the corners of his mouth, revealing the tops of pink gums.

"But not that big." Elizabeth had been told by the sales representative that they should look cheerful and that their hands should be clean at all times. Customers didn't want to handle dirty money.

"OK." He relaxed his smile until his gums disappeared beneath his lip.

Elizabeth rang the doorbell, which *ding-donged* loud and clear. After a few seconds Leonard rang the doorbell with his thumb, pressing hard, the way he did to kill ants. They waited with their hands at their sides. Admiring a rose near the steps, Elizabeth lowered her face and sniffed its fragrance.

"It smells pretty," she said. "You try."

Leonard pushed his small face right into the flower and two petals fell off. He picked them up and sniffed so that the suction plastered them to his nose. But the petals dropped when Elizabeth tugged on his arm.

She rang the bell a third time. It seemed that no one was home but when they had turned to leave, a voice said, "I'm glad you've come."

They looked at a woman standing by the side gate. She was elderly, and her gray hair was tinted blue. She seemed nervous, almost scared. She beckoned them over with a wave of an age-spotted hand.

Elizabeth started her sales pitch: "Good afternoon,

señora. We're offering a line of delicious peanut brittle and mints—"

The woman cut her off. "You have to help me. They won't leave!"

"*¿Señora?*" Elizabeth asked, confused.

"The squirrels. They won't leave."

"The lady has squirrels?" Leonard asked, looking up to his sister.

"Quiet, Lenny," Elizabeth said.

"You must help me, *por favor, niños*," the woman pleaded.

She opened the gate and the children, without thinking, entered and followed her to the backyard, where more roses bloomed brightly. The woman took the two children to the patio door and said, "They're by the recliner."

"Who's by the recliner?" Elizabeth asked. To Leonard she said, "You don't have to smile anymore."

Leonard relaxed his face and turned to a plum tree weighed down with fruit. He wanted to race over to the tree, but he knew better. It wasn't his tree.

"The squirrels," the woman panted. "They came in yesterday. I tried to get them out, but they won't go. I had to sleep in the garage."

"*Señora*, we're selling candy. I don't know anything about squirrels."

"I will buy what you have," the woman promised. She twisted a handkerchief in her hand. On one finger, a diamond sparkled, giving off a blue, cool light.

"Are you sure? They cost four dollars a box."

Leonard held up four sticky fingers.

"I'll pay if you help me. My purse is inside, in my bedroom."

Elizabeth cupped her hands around her eyes and peered into the house. She saw the recliner but no squirrels. She turned to the woman and asked, "How did they get in?"

"I left the patio door open. They just came in."

With a deep breath and a "here goes" attitude, Elizabeth opened the patio door and walked into the house. The only sound was the drip in the sink and the buzz of flies. Then the refrigerator kicked in, humming.

"You stay there," Elizabeth warned Leonard, turning around. To the woman she said, "I'll chase them out with a broom."

"I don't have a broom inside. It's in the garage."

"Well, I'll find something," Elizabeth said. She entered the house; it reminded her of her grandmother's house. On the dark paneled walls hung pictures of happy and sad clowns and the Kennedys, a ceramic chicken, a seascape, and a dried grapevine wreath. The plastic flowers on the end table were sticky with dust. Old newspapers were piled in a corner. A row of cacti in sawed-off milk cartons stood on a makeshift shelf, figurines of boys and girls poking out between them.

Elizabeth put her plastic bag of peanut brittle and mints down on the rocker and picked up one of the figurines. It was a boy with rosy cheeks and a chipped nose.

"How cute," she said, smiling.

She put it back when she spotted a fishbowl. A fish was twisting in the green water; it seemed near death, its mouth pouting and its eyes locked on nothing. The fish must be dying from the heat, Elizabeth thought.

She was startled when she heard a rustle in the kitchen. She reached for a yardstick that had been left on the TV and approached the noise cautiously. When she looked in the kitchen, she saw a squirrel on its haunches, nibbling from a bag of spaghetti that had spilled on the floor. He had a strand of spaghetti between his tiny paws; it looked like he was holding a spear.

"Shoo!" Elizabeth yelled. She stomped her foot, crying, "Go! Get outta here!"

The squirrel kept chewing.

"Get outta here! Beat it!" she repeated, raising the yardstick and slapping it against the refrigerator. A few scraps of paper fell to the floor, along with a magnetic flashlight. The squirrel dropped its spaghetti and leapt into the living room, where it hid underneath the recliner, its puffed tail still in view. Elizabeth tiptoed past the recliner and opened the front door, hoping the squirrel would run out. She spied the shirtless neighbor on his front porch across the street, arguing with his wife.

Elizabeth wheeled around and saw another squirrel standing in the dark hallway. At the clap of her hands, the squirrel scampered down the hallway into one of the bedrooms.

"Darn it," Elizabeth hissed. She took a chocolate kiss from the candy dish. This is going to be hard, she thought. She ate the candy and then had another, wondering why the lady would be scared of squirrels. They were so harmless, she thought, and cute.

Finally Elizabeth tiptoed toward the bedroom, the yardstick poised in her hand like a sword. She stopped at the half-closed door and, after composing herself with three deep breaths, pushed it open with the yardstick. When she looked in the bedroom, Elizabeth nearly screamed at the sight of a huge, fuzzy brown thing slouching on the ruffled bed—until she realized it was a stuffed bear as big as her brother and just as brown.

It must have been the woman's daughter's room, Elizabeth thought. She flicked on the lights and scanned the bedroom, looking from left to right and from top to bottom. A row of dusty tennis trophies lined a shelf, and in the midst of the trophies stood one of the squirrels, looking at her with liquid eyes.

"Get down!" she yelled. But the squirrel didn't move. It stared at Elizabeth until she became frightened and hurried out of the room. She went back to the patio, where the woman and Leonard were peering into the house, their faces plastered to the glass of the patio door.

"*Señora*," she said, "it's hard. Those squirrels won't behave."

"I will buy all your candies and give you ten dollars more." The woman's face was desperate. Her hands were twisting the handkerchief.

"*Señora*," Elizabeth said after clearing her throat, "I'm going to try one more time. But I need you to come inside."

"I can't *stand* squirrels," the woman said, her voice quivering.

"They're kinda cute."

"They're not cute. They're rats with big tails."

"Well, I chased one. It went into the bedroom."

"Into my daughter's bedroom?"

"The room with the stuffed bear."

The woman started crying. "That's my daughter's bedroom. I never hear from her anymore." She sniffled. "I'm tired. I had to sleep in the garage last night."

Elizabeth sighed. Without saying anything she went back inside. The room seemed hotter and the air was filled with the drone of flies that had come in through the front door. She heard a rustling sound. She took a slow step, the yardstick raised, and when she turned her gaze to the rocker, she saw that one of the squirrels had ripped open a box and was now holding a card of peanut brittle in its tiny paws.

"If you're gonna eat it, you're going to pay for it!" Elizabeth screamed, angry at last. She raised the yardstick and brought it down hard on the arm of the rocker. The squirrel bolted and the peanut brittle fell to the floor and shattered.

"You little runt," she yelled, running after the squirrel, which returned to the daughter's bedroom. Elizabeth hesitated at the door of the bedroom. "Come out, you little thief." The squirrel didn't come out, so Elizabeth stepped into the room and swung the yardstick like a sword. She hit the chest of drawers. Both squirrels had been sitting on the bed; they separated and scampered up the curtains. Elizabeth beat the curtains, and they jumped to the face of the stuffed bear, where they hunkered and stared up at her. She whacked the bear's belly, which gave up a cloud of dust. The squirrels leapt out of the bedroom and fled up the hallway toward the front door.

"Get outta here!" Elizabeth yelled, slapping the side of the wall with the yardstick. A family portrait fell to the floor, face down. She slapped the yardstick again, and a straw basket fell, followed by a mirror with faint lettering that said Let the Sun Shine In. She kicked the basket out of the way and stepped over the mirror. She rushed around the corner and screamed when she was confronted by the man from across the street. He was scratching his tattooed belly threateningly. "What are you doing?" he asked. "Does Mrs. Garcia know you're here? Did you break in?"

Elizabeth took a step backward, trembling. "I'm helping get rid of her squirrels," she said feebly.

"What squirrels?" he asked.

"These two squirrels that came into the house." Elizabeth realized that she sounded wacky. "Mrs. Garcia had to sleep out in the garage. The squirrels won't leave her alone."

"Yeah, sure," he said suspiciously. The man started toward Elizabeth, and she jumped and ran away, on the verge of tears. She tossed away the yardstick, grabbed her bag of candies, and ran out to the patio, where Leonard was in the tree eating plums.

"*Señora*, I can't help you," she shouted, and to her sticky-faced brother, who knew something was up, she called, "Leonard, get down!"

"You have to!" the woman cried.

"I won't."

The woman collapsed in a wicker chair, pressing her handkerchief to her face and muttering, "Oh, I wish my daughter would call . . ."

Leonard dropped from the tree and was at Elizabeth's side in a flash. "Did you get 'em?" he asked.

"Shut up," Elizabeth snapped, tugging on his arm.

The two children took off past the side of the house. In the front yard the man yelled for them to stop; he wanted to buy a box of mints and one of the coloring books. But they didn't stop. They ran with their feet kicking high for two blocks. They slowed only when a squirrel jumped from a tree and stood begging in their path. Elizabeth shouted at the squirrel to leave them alone, and they ran two more blocks. They slowed to a walk, sweating, and sat on the curb, where they opened a box of mints and studied the coloring books full of heroes no one had ever heard about.

THE MECHANICAL MIND

PHILIP QUINTANA DISCOVERED that he was mechanical on a hot summer day when he took a pair of pliers, climbed to the roof of his house with a boost from his younger sister, Leticia, and straightened the kinked tubing that fed water to their evaporator cooler. He opened the sides of the cooler and, peering in, studied the small greasy motor, its fan belt jumping violently as it turned the cagelike fan.

The pads were rotted, black as a diseased lung. They crumbled when he poked the pliers at them and gave off a musty smell from the years of water that had dribbled over them. Remembering the new pads stored in the garage, Philip tore the old ones out and, holding his breath, jumped off the roof. He landed with a groan but got up brushing grass from his palms. He fetched the new pads and, with the help once again of his sister, who complained that he was too heavy, Philip climbed to the roof.

"Higher, Leti," he yelled at his sister, who was trying to fling the new pads onto the roof. But Leticia was only seven and too weak to throw the pads high enough for Philip to catch them. Eventually a high school student riding by on his dirt bike stopped and flung the pads to the roof, and then Philip was able to get to work. And the work was easy. The pads were crisp as shredded wheat, and in a matter of minutes Philip, whistling away, was able to tuck them into the walls of the cooler.

"All right," he said, admiring his handiwork. He slapped his hands clean and jumped off the roof with the old pads, one in each hand. He heaved the pads into the alley and paraded into the house with his sister in tow.

"Smells good," Philip said, breathing in the smell of new cooler pads.

"Smells funny," his sister said. She stood under the vent that threw out the cool air. "It smells like when you sharpen pencils."

"Mom and Dad are gonna be surprised."

Their parents were at work, and because Philip was twelve and going into the seventh grade, he was expected to take care of his sister.

"Let's have lunch," Philip suggested. He washed his hands at the kitchen sink and made bologna-and-cheese sandwiches for his sister and for himself. They took their sandwiches, along with an orange soda to share, and sat at the kitchen table. Philip fed off his sandwich and the discovery that he was mechanically minded. Right then, as he ate, Philip got it into his head that he would look inside the telephone hanging on the wall. He ate quickly and then used a screwdriver to pop off the plastic front of the telephone.

"You're gonna get in trouble," Leticia said, her mouth full and her face greasy from the sandwich.

"No, I'm not," Philip replied. "If it breaks, I'll just fix it. I have a mechanical mind." He strummed the bunched strands of red and yellow wires, then put his ear to the receiver. The telephone still worked.

"See," he said when he dialed his best friend, Ricky, and got Ricky's mother, who answered, "*Bueno.*" He hung up and said, "It ain't broke."

His curiosity satisfied, Philip replaced the face of the telephone and decided to open the back of the clock radio in his parents' bedroom. Ever since his father had knocked it over while putting a new light bulb in the lamp by the bed, the radio had hummed. Now Philip would see what was wrong. He unscrewed the back and lifted the top, discovering a simple network of circuits and wires. There were also clots of dust and a mysterious toothpick lodged inside. He blew away the dust and used the end of his T-shirt to clean the corners. He was surprised at the tiny puddles of solder and the fishline device that changed the stations. The humming miraculously stopped. Philip stood, hands on hips, feeling proud.

"See, it don't buzz no more," he said to his sister.

Leticia lowered her ear to the radio. The buzzing had indeed stopped.

Perched on their parents' end table, along with the radio, was a bottle of moisturizing lotion with a pump. Philip pressed the pump, and a yellowish lotion oozed into his hand. He rubbed it into his face, some of it sticking to his eyelashes.

"The lotion works like this," Philip started. "You see the pump—it works like gravity, like when astronauts jump on the moon. You probably don't understand, Leti, because you're not mechanically minded."

Leticia looked at her brother with new respect. She had never heard talk like this. She pumped a dimple of lotion into one palm, pressed her hands together, and then rubbed it on her arms.

Next Philip unscrewed the hair dryer. He looked at the wires and the small motor encased in hard plastic. He explained to his awed sister that an electric fire was created in the motor and then air was trapped in a chamber that exploded every two or three seconds. "That's how your head heats up," he reasoned. He flicked on the hair dryer, and Leticia ran from the bathroom, her hands covering her head, screaming, "Don't burn my hair!"

Feeling more ambitious, Philip decided he would take apart the microwave oven. First he microwaved an ice cube and explained to Leticia that the waves were radar that could zap water from a stone.

"Go ahead and drink it," Philip dared Leticia as he shoved a cup of melted ice at her. Steam was rising from the near-boiling water.

"No way!" Leticia yelled. "And you better not mess with the microwave. Mom'll kill you."

But it was too late. Philip's screwdriver slipped and scraped off a piece of the imitation-wood facing. He decided to leave the microwave oven alone.

"Well, it was getting too old," he said. "Some of the radar leaked out and hurt the paint."

"Radar?" Leticia asked. "You're making this up."

"Radar heats the food," he said, feeling insulted that his mechanical mind was being doubted by a seven-year-old. "It's a proven fact. That's how astronauts heat up their grub in space."

Leticia looked up at her brother, again awed.

Then Philip remembered their television's lousy reception. He hurried to the living room with his screwdriver and studied the large, beastlike console, a gift from his grandmother, who had won it in a drawing at the bingo parlor. He turned it on and heard TV laughter as a clear picture came into view. A game show host was standing on his head.

"Is the TV upside down?" Leticia asked. Her mouth was stuffed with an Oreo cookie that blackened her front teeth.

"He's being stupid," Philip answered. "Leti, I'm going to climb the roof and adjust the antenna. I think that's the problem."

"I'm not going to help you up. You're too heavy."

"Just tell me when the picture is clear, OK?" he asked as he walked out the front door.

The afternoon heat created a mirage of water wavering on the street. On tiptoes, one hand cupped like a salute over his brow, Philip eyed the roof. The antenna, leaning slightly, stood right over the living room.

Using a ladder he had retrieved from behind the garage, Philip climbed onto the roof. He remembered his father saying that the television's reception could be adjusted by turning the antenna clockwise. Philip spit into his palms and turned the antenna, which bobbed softly as a tree branch.

"Is it better?" he yelled to Leticia.

"No," she yelled, her voice rising powerfully through the roof.

He turned it again and yelled, "How 'bout now?"

"No, it's really bad."

Sweating from the summer heat, Philip groaned and rotated the antenna, which began to shake and lean even more. "How 'bout now?"

"It's all weird."

Confused, Philip jumped off the roof. He was going to see for himself. He smashed a snail with the heel of one palm when he landed on the grass, but he didn't have time to get disgusted. It was time to put his mechanical mind to work. He went inside and saw that the television picture was a zigzag of colors. Philip watched the commercial. To him it looked like a woman was shampooing her hair with blue fire.

"It's makin' me sick," Leticia whined. She put her Oreo down on the coffee table and covered her mouth with both hands. She was getting ready to lose her sandwich and cookies—maybe even some of her breakfast.

Philip had to agree that the TV picture was sickening. He turned off the television, waited a few seconds, and then turned the set back on. The screen was still a zigzag of colors and long, frightful faces.

"Stupid thing," he scolded, pounding the television.

The faces flickered but wouldn't fatten into regular human features. Philip wouldn't give up. He told Leticia, "I'm goin' to try again."

He climbed the ladder again but was having doubts. Maybe I'm not mechanically minded, he thought. He slipped on the roof and clutched at the grainy shingles so he wouldn't slide off. He got back to his feet, one knee bleeding, and leaned as he walked, as if he were trudging through a blizzard. He took the antenna in his hands and turned it clockwise, just as his father had explained.

"How is it now?" he yelled.

"I think the man is standing on his head again," Leticia yelled back.

"How 'bout now?"

"It's really bad."

"Now?"

"Everyone's orange."

Philip rotated the antenna until a clamp snapped and the antenna fell like a tree, striking the cooler and splitting the copper tubing he had repaired only an hour ago.

Philip's mouth fell open as he watched the water rush over the roof and off the eaves like a waterfall.

"It's working!" he heard his sister squeal. He could imagine her jumping up and down. "The TV is working. The guy is standing on his feet." His sister laughed and screamed through the roof, "Phil, you have a mechanical mind!"

ℵICKEL-A-POUND PLANE RIDE

ARACELI SLIPPED THE RUBBER BAND off the morning newspaper. One eye closed, she shot it across the living room at her sleeping cat, Asco, who didn't stir.

"You lazy thing," Araceli muttered, smiling and pushing her long hair behind her ears. Araceli was a slightly built twelve-year-old, skin the color of brown sugar, eyes shiny with triangles of light. She could wiggle a little of her tongue in the gap between her front teeth.

She unfolded the newspaper and glanced at the front page. She grimaced at a photo of a car wreck on Highway 99. It was winter in California's San Joaquin Valley; cold air burned like ice pressed against a warm cheek, and sometimes the fog and rain caused cars to slide off the freeway and buckle like aluminum cans.

But this morning Araceli didn't care about the front

page. Her friend Carolina had called last night with more exciting news: she had heard about some airplane rides at Chandler Airfield for almost nothing. More than anything Araceli wanted to fly in an airplane. Everyone she knew had gone up in a plane and come down like an angel. Her mother and father had flown to Hawaii for their tenth wedding anniversary. Her grandfather flew to Reno once a month. Her cousin, who was the manager of a rock group, spent more time airborne between pillowy clouds than on the black asphalt of Los Angeles, his hometown. Her brother, Eddie, a junior in high school and the drum major for the Roosevelt High School marching band, had flown to New York to be in the Macy's Parade. Even her baby cousin, Carlos, had flown from Los Angeles to Guadalajara, shaking a yellow rattle for hours, he was so happy.

Settling into the couch Araceli scoured the paper for news of the plane rides. Toward the back of the paper near the gardening section, wedged between the black-and-white ads for tri-tips and lawn mowers, her eye caught the one-column story: the American Legion was offering nickel-a-pound airplane rides to benefit the Children's Hospital.

"Finally," Araceli beamed, rereading the story two more times. "I'm going to fly!" She spread her arms like wings and flew into the kitchen, where she fixed herself a bowl of cornflakes and made some coffee. Instead of milk, Araceli poured coffee laced with a splash of cream over her cereal, a concoction she'd learned about from her grandmother. She liked the taste of hot coffee over soggy cornflakes—and she liked the idea that she was grown up enough to drink coffee.

Her father came into the kitchen looking for the newspaper. His hair was tousled, and his eyes glazed from a hard sleep.

"Morning, Dad," Araceli greeted him, not looking up from the comics. She automatically handed him the sports section.

"Morning, sugar," he said groggily, taking the section and staggering to the kitchen counter, where he poured coffee into his Raiders cup. He took the paper and coffee into the living room.

Araceli rinsed her bowl at the sink and straightened the newspaper. She knew she had to be extra good because she was going to beg her dad to take her to Chandler Airfield. She danced into the living room and asked, "Dad, do you want another cup of coffee?"

Still reading his newspaper, her father held out his half-empty cup. She took it to the kitchen and carefully measured out the hot black brew from their Mr. Coffee, poured in a dash of half-and-half, and brought the cup back to him.

"Dad," Araceli said, after he'd pursed his lips and sipped his coffee with a quiet slurp. "Dad, we should do something special this weekend."

Having turned to the front section of the paper, her father was reading about the freeway accident. "Yeah, you can clean up your room. Mom will be home this evening." Araceli's mother was on a retreat in the mountains with other women from church.

"It's clean already."

"Clean it some more." A smile played at the corners of her father's mouth. He was kidding her.

"No, Dad, I want to go flying."

Her father put down the paper and gave Araceli a baffled look. He touched her forehead and asked playfully, "Do you have a fever?"

"Dad," she wheedled. "Dad, they have this thing where you can pay a nickel for every pound you weigh and then you get to fly."

"You're gonna make me poor."

"I'm not fat." She knew she was halfway to convincing her father.

"Well, tell me more about this plane ride," her father said.

"We're helping the world," Araceli explained. "The money goes to Children's Hospital. Think of all the babies we will save if we go and get on the plane. The American Legion will be able to buy all these machines, and then everybody will be OK."

Her father laughed. "How much do you weigh? They're gonna make a fortune off you."

"Every little bit helps."

"You're funny," her father said. "I'm going to shave. We'll go—*ahorita*."

"All right!" Araceli yelled, jumping up and down and twirling so that her nightie flared.

Araceli went into the bathroom and, still wearing her flannel nightgown printed with horses, stood on the cold scale. She weighed sixty-eight pounds. She stood on tiptoe, hoping it would make her weigh less. The needle twitched, but her weight remained the same.

Father and daughter dressed for the day.

"It's gonna rain buckets, I think," Araceli's father said, stepping out onto the porch. The wind was shaking the top of the elm in front of their house. The sky was as gray as cement. The neighbor's chimney was sending up billows of smoke that immediately broke apart in the wind.

They settled into the Honda and drove west toward Chandler Airfield, which was at the edge of town. Araceli's father turned on the headlights and swished the wipers to clear the mist from the windshield. The heater warmed their feet.

"Are you sure you want to fly?" he asked. He wasn't teasing her now. He peered through the windshield at the dark sky. A few drops of rain blurred the glass.

"I'm not scared," Araceli said, smiling stiffly at her father. She worked her tongue into the gap between her front teeth. She wanted to fly; she was determined to do it.

As they approached the airfield, they spotted a single-engine airplane taking off. It seemed effortless: a short run on the airstrip, and then it was up, up, up.

The mist had become a soft, slanting rain. Araceli and her father got out of the car and—hand-in-gloved-hand, their jacket hoods over their heads—hurried across the parking lot to the long line of people waiting to fly.

After a few minutes in line her father said, "I don't know, sugar."

"Come on, Dad. It's not that long."

"Not long? There's only two planes and all these people."

To the west, a feather of blue was showing between the dark clouds.

"See, it might even clear up," Araceli argued, pointing to that faraway blue sky.

A few people in line gave up and raced back to their cars. The line stepped ahead like a centipede. Araceli's father, shuddering from the cold, suggested, "I have an idea. You can wait in the car and I'll wait in line. We'll take turns every ten minutes." He looked down at his watch. "It's fifteen to twelve."

Araceli nodded. "Fair enough."

She raced back to the car, leaping over puddles, and immediately flicked on the heater. She held her hands up to the vents and sneezed.

She stayed in the car for exactly eight minutes and then raced back to the line. She was surprised how wet her father looked. The hood of his jacket was plastered to his head, and his eyeglasses were so splattered with rain that he couldn't see her clearly enough to recognize her. She had to tug on his arm to get his attention.

"Dad, it's me."

"Sugar, it's really starting to come down," he said.

"It's not that bad."

"It is. The man said they might cancel the flights."

"Come on, Dad."

A large family in front of them gave up, in spite of tantrums from two of the children. They hurried back to their station wagon, and suddenly Araceli was almost to the gate.

"You go. I'll wait for you," her father said.

"Come on, Dad," Araceli insisted.

"I weigh too much," he chuckled. "I didn't bring the checkbook."

At that moment Araceli's friend, Carolina, walked slowly out of the gate clinging to her father's arm. They had just landed with the latest load of passengers.

"Carolina," Araceli shouted through cupped hands. "How was it?"

Carolina looked in Araceli's direction but didn't say anything. Her eyes seemed shiny, as if she had gotten a lot of rain in them.

"What's wrong with her?" Araceli asked her father.

"Maybe she's sick. I'm getting cold."

"I'm not cold," Araceli lied. "In fact, I'm hot." She undid the top button of her jacket.

When they were finally next in line, her father turned to Araceli and said, "You can change your mind."

"No way," she said. She hopped up on the scale and smiled at her weight: 74 pounds, wet clothes and all. "See, Dad, I'm not fat."

Her father paid and was given a stub that declared his donation to be tax deductible.

"Hold on," Araceli heard her father say, but the advice that followed was eaten by the wind. A man ushered her to the airplane, where a man, woman, and boy sat waiting.

Araceli climbed on board next to the boy. She was glad to get out of the rain and wind, but she was shocked by how small the compartment was. There was hardly room for her to move her feet. Even the airplane's windshield was small, like a little picture frame.

"Buckle your seat belts," the pilot said.

Araceli strapped herself in and smiled. She stopped smiling as the engine began to roar. The noise was deafening. She held her gloved hands over her ears and saw that the other passengers were doing the same. They were large, couch-potato types, and they all smelled of wet wool. She wondered how much it had cost that family to fly, and then she wondered if the airplane could get off the ground with all that weight.

"This is going to be fun," she said over the roar of the engine.

The boy looked doubtfully at Araceli.

The airplane maneuvered onto the runway. Araceli leaned forward between the mother and father opposite her. She wanted to get a peek at the pilot turning knobs, flicking switches, and adjusting levers. She saw him pull back the throttle, and the airplane began to fishtail down the runway.

The plane seemed to move slowly, and for the first time Araceli worried that they might crash. She wished that these heavy people were not on board. She was upset by the thought that, if the plane crashed, she would be squashed like a bug under their weight.

Araceli closed her eyes and tried to get a sense of when the airplane left the ground. She wanted to memorize this sensation. She wanted to write in her diary later, "I was off the ground, and it was cool."

But when she opened her eyes, she discovered that they were still rolling down the runway. She screamed, "Come on, get us in the air."

The boy and his parents looked at Araceli. They looked like turtles, slow, with unblinking eyes. The pilot didn't turn his head.

The airplane bumped twice on the runway, and then they were airborne, the wings tipping left, then right, as the airplane climbed.

I'm flying, Araceli thought. She made the sign of the cross and muttered, "I'm not scared."

The airplane dipped and rocked, and Araceli's face slammed into the boy's shoulder. He turned and looked at Araceli but didn't say a word.

"Hold on to your hats," the pilot said calmly. "Winds are out of the northwest."

The airplane vibrated and shuddered, and everyone except the pilot screamed when it bumped through an air pocket. Araceli made the sign of the cross a second time as she closed her eyes to pray. When she opened her eyes, blinking slowly because it all seemed like a dream, she saw a patch of blue in the distance. She thought she might be in heaven, until she smelled the wet coats of the couch potatoes. This is not heaven, she thought.

The plane rocked again, and the left wing dipped. Araceli recalled the roller coaster she'd ridden in Santa Cruz, a big wooden structure called the Big Dipper. She had been nine at the time and foolish—so foolish that when the roller coaster sped earthward, she had closed her eyes and screamed. The wind had ripped the gum out of her wide-open mouth and tore a dollar bill from her fingers.

But now she was four thousand feet above her hometown. She was twelve, not nine, and still she was scared.

The turtle-faced boy and his parents mumbled among themselves. They fumbled with their seat belts, and the father, leaning into the pilot's shoulder, asked, "These doors got locks?"

The pilot laughed, "No, of course not," and gripped the controls as the plane shuddered. "There's nothing to worry about."

Araceli wondered if the airplane was equipped with parachutes. She looked around. She saw only an old orange T-shirt. If only I could find some string, she thought. I could make my own parachute.

When the airplane banked right, Araceli slid into the corner. The pilot pointed out landmarks: the Fresno Convention Center, the water tower, Kearny Park. The stadium stood out in the distance, its lights on as evidence of taxpayers' money being wasted. He spotted a wreck on Highway 99.

The pilot pointed with his gloved hand, but Araceli couldn't see the landmarks from the back of the plane. She stared at the back of the woman's jacket and began to feel better. She thought that if they crashed, she would be cushioned by this family's big jackets. She would survive the crash and tell about it on TV.

Araceli once again saw a patch of blue sky. She pointed

a finger and screamed over the engine noise to the pilot, "Can't you fly over there?"

"What?" he yelled back.

"Don't you think it's better over there?" The blue patch was slowly filling with gray clouds. "Never mind." She fell back in her seat, chewed on a fingernail, and crossed herself for the third time.

They circled once and then returned for landing. Araceli began to pray in earnest as the airplane kept wiggling and dropped suddenly.

"Hold on," the pilot warned. His sunglasses had slid crookedly across his face.

The airplane landed safely, and Araceli was glad that she got away with just a few jolts. She couldn't hear because the sound of the engine continued to play over and over in her ears.

She jumped from the cockpit without thanking the pilot or even glancing at her traveling companions, who were shaking out their stiff legs. She raced to her father and hugged him, hard.

"How was it, sugar?" he asked, drinking coffee from a Styrofoam cup.

"Great! I love flying." She tried to climb into his arms, but her father took her by the hand and walked her back to the car. She was glad when the car got going and the heater blew hot air on her cold toes. She took off her socks and shoes and saw that her toes were wrinkled, as if she had stayed in the bathtub too long.

They returned home to find Araceli's mother doing aerobics to oldies music.

"Hi, Mom, I went flying," Araceli yelled. She threw her arms around her mother's waist and said, "I missed you."

Her mother turned down the volume on the stereo. "You went flying?"

"Yeah, it was a special thing. We were helping children who are sick."

"You weren't scared?"

"Of course not!"

She explained the nickel-a-pound airplane rides and the beautiful sensations of flying. She didn't tell her mother about the burly family of three.

Araceli took a hot bath and lounged around the house, occasionally hugging her father, then her mother, then Asco. She even smiled at her brother, who had come home wet as a duck after playing football with his friends.

As she watched TV Araceli gripped the arms of the chair. When a United Airlines commercial came on, she changed the channel. She didn't want to think about flying—she wanted to think about being on the ground.

She ate dinner and went to bed early. Nestled safely in bed she said some more prayers and thought about the rain in Carolina's eyes. They were tears, she realized, and then, to her surprise, Araceli began to cry big, hot, nickel-sized tears. Flying was no fun at all.

new Year's Eve

EARLY IN THE DAY ten-year-old Blanca Mendoza had walked three blocks to her cousin's house, where they'd played soccer in the front yard until the ball hit Blanca square in the face. She'd gone down, a hand clapped to her cheek, and started crying. From a distance someone might have thought she was pretending to be a cow. Her crying sounded like "*moo-moo, moo-moo.*"

"Oh, Blanca, I'm sorry. You OK?" her cousin Dulce had asked, bending down on one knee to soothe her. Dulce was afraid she would get in trouble if her mother looked out the front window.

Blanca wiped away the hot tears and got to her feet, sniffing back her sobs. She wiped loose blades of grass off her hands and said to Dulce, "It wasn't your fault."

"Let's do something else," Dulce suggested, trying to

cheer Blanca up by looking happy. "You want to play Sears?"

Sears was a game they'd invented: they went through the Sears catalogue, choosing toys they liked—Nintendo, battery-powered squirt guns, Barbie dolls, Game Boys, bicycles. First it would be Blanca's turn, then Dulce's, then Blanca's, then Dulce's, until all the good toys were chosen and it was time to turn the page.

"No, I'm going home," Blanca said.

"Are you mad?" Dulce asked.

"No," she snapped.

But she *was* mad, although not at Dulce. She was mad at her father. He had promised to take her to the snow but at the last minute, he had been called away to tow a car from the freeway. He owned Ray's Towing Service, and business was business. He had to go when the telephone rang, even if today was New Year's Eve and even if he'd promised to take his daughter to the snow.

Blanca had waited weeks for the trip, lining her tennis shoes with plastic sandwich bags to keep her feet dry. She had cut and snipped sandwich bags and fit them into her wool gloves, too. Blanca knew that snow stung like fire, but she was eager to trudge knee-deep in it and slide down the hills, face first, on an inner tube.

Now Blanca was at home, licking the sides of her mouth. Her mother had fixed her a cup of hot chocolate, and, feeling almost happy, Blanca was on the couch looking out the front window. The valley fog pressed up to the glass. It was so foggy that Blanca couldn't make out the cherry-red Chevy parked on the lawn across the street.

"It's so *feo*," Blanca's mother said, throwing a sweater over her shoulders. "I hope your father is OK."

Blanca didn't say anything. She got up on her knees and watched a cat slink toward a robin hopping across the lawn. Blanca banged on the window with the heel of her palm. The bird, a writhing worm in its beak, looked in her direction and, sensing danger, leapt skyward as the cat pounced.

"You bad cat," Blanca called, wagging a finger at the animal. The cat looked mad, with one of its fangs sticking out of its mouth.

Her father's tow truck pulled noisily into the driveway, and the cat took off toward the bushes. "Dad's home!" Blanca shouted to her mother, who was in the kitchen. Blanca bounced from the couch and scrambled to the door. She opened it with a tug and, walking out onto the cold porch with no shoes, yelled, "Dad, can we go now?"

She hoped they would still have time to go to the snow. The drive would only take an hour. Since it was two o'clock, she figured that they could get there by three and there would be enough time to slide a dozen times down the slope and still get home in time for dinner.

But seeing her father's slow walk, Blanca knew that he would say no, that he was tired and wanted to relax in front of the TV.

"Hi, Dad," she greeted him.

Her father, climbing the steps, said, "Honey, it's cold. Better get inside."

They went in together, her soft hand in her father's rough, oil-darkened hand. It was just as she had thought: he went to the kitchen, poured himself a cup of coffee, and said to her mother, "*Hace mucho frío.*" He plopped into his recliner, zapped on the television, and tuned in to a football game.

"Dad," Blanca started. "Dad, you said we were going to the snow . . ."

Her father turned his dark face to her. "*Mi'ja*, tomorrow. It's cold today, and late." He looked at her for a second and then turned his head to the television when he heard the crowd roar for a touchdown.

"You promise?" she asked.

"I promise," he said.

"And you promise I can stay up until midnight?"

"I promise," he said, looking at the TV.

"Sure," Blanca mumbled, not believing her father. She went to her bedroom. She felt like crying, but she had already had a good cry on Dulce's front lawn. So she threw herself on her ruffled bed, opened the Sears catalogue, and looked at the pictures of toys until she was called to dinner.

"We will stay up till midnight," her father said, cutting an enchilada with his fork. "We will stay up and drink champagne."

"*Viejo*, we don't have champagne," Blanca's mother said.

"Then I will drink a beer. We must be a little dizzy for the coming year." Her father was happy. He had been saying for months that 1993 would be the year when his

135

towing service would really take off and they would get rich.

"Can I stay up, too?" Blanca asked. She was balancing a pile of *fideo* on her fork, cooling the noodles.

"*¿Cómo no?*" her father said. "You can find out what mice do when we're asleep."

Blanca had never stayed up past 9:00 P.M. except once. One time they had gone to the Sunnyside Drive-In to see *Robin Hood*. No matter how hard she had tried to stay awake, her head had kept nodding sleepily. Eventually she'd slumped over like a teddy bear in her mother's arms. But she did wake up on the drive home and had looked out the frosty window into the night sky. She'd found a cluster of three stars and a quarter moon that rode the sky beyond a line of dark trees.

They ate dinner and watched television. But when Blanca saw her father yawn and stretch, she said, "*Papi*, you promised."

His eyes were watery, distant. He patted her arm and said, "Oh, yes, we must celebrate." He sat straight up in his recliner, then turned his attention to the television. But Blanca could see he was too tired to celebrate, and she could see her mother on the couch reading a nursing book. She was taking two classes at City College, and her books were thick and difficult. Her mother yawned, took off her eyeglasses, and began to rub her face.

"You, too, Mom," Blanca said. "You said you'd stay up."

"*Mi'ja, estoy cansada.* I had a long day."

"I did, too. Dulce kicked a ball in my face." Blanca

touched her cheek, rubbing gently as if she were soothing it with lotion.

"*¿Qué?*"

"Nothing." Blanca didn't want to tell on her cousin— and what was there to tell, anyway? It had been an accident. "Mom, you promised you'd stay up!"

"Sweetheart, I'm exhausted."

"How 'bout if I make you some hot chocolate?"

"It's getting late. I'm sleepy."

So was Blanca's father, who had nodded off and was snoring gently in his recliner.

"I'm going to bed," her mother said, placing her book on the end table. She got up, turned off the television, and went to the kitchen to lock the back door. Blanca was furious. With her mother out of sight, she got up and took the large nursing book. She tiptoed toward her sleeping father and, hovering over him, opened the book, slammed it shut, and dropped it to the floor.

"*¡Ay, Dios!*" he screamed, his eyes popping open.

"The book fell, Dad," Blanca explained simply. "Sorry. Are you going to stay up?"

Her father looked around, lost. He sat up in his recliner, shook off his fear, and said, "I'm going to bed."

"Dad!" Blanca nearly screamed. "You said we were going to greet the New Year. You said we can find out what the mice do."

Blanca's mother returned and snapped, "Blanca, don't raise your voice. Dad is tired. If you want to stay up, fine."

"I will," Blanca grumbled as she picked up the nursing

book from the floor. Her feelings were hurt. She promised herself that she would stay up, even if her parents were in bed—and that's where they went, leaving Blanca in the living room feeling sad. She went into the kitchen and looked at the clock; it was ten after nine.

"I'm going to call Dulce," she said, scooting a chair over to the telephone on the kitchen wall. She dialed and got her aunt Sylvia, Dulce's mother.

"Auntie, it's me," Blanca said.

"Blanca?" her aunt asked. "Is something wrong?"

"No. I just wanted to say hi to Dulce."

"She's in bed, pumpkin. Why aren't you in bed?"

"It's New Year's Eve. I'm staying up until twelve."

"You're going to be tired tomorrow."

"Tell Dulce that I stayed up till twelve."

"I will. But you get to bed soon."

"Bye, Auntie." Blanca hung up and jumped down from the chair, feeling a flower of happiness unfolding inside her. Dulce was in bed, and so were Blanca's parents. She rubbed her hands together like a fly. She decided to make herself a sandwich. She opened the refrigerator and took out her father's favorite lunch meat, turkey. She added a wedge of tomato, a cheese slice, and mustard. She climbed on the chair again to get the bag of corn chips from the top of the refrigerator.

Blanca carried her sandwich—along with the chips, a stout pickle, and a glass of milk—to the living room. She sat in her dad's recliner and zapped on the television. She kept the sound turned low because she didn't want her parents to tell her to go to bed. A car salesman with no hair flashed on the television screen. She changed the channel and watched another commercial, this one showing a woman before and after a weight-loss program.

"Gross," Blanca said.

She switched to another channel, and faces appeared and disappeared like playing cards being shuffled. Finally she settled on a movie that looked like it might be scary. A man was half-dead on a beach, the side of his face swollen. Sure enough, it was a scary movie. A sea creature the color of a rusty radiator was after the man. Blanca liked being scared, and she ate her sandwich in nine big bites, like the sea creature that first devoured one man and then another who was trying to save the first man.

Blanca wondered what was it like to be eaten. She had read somewhere that a girl fell through a fence onto the alligators' island at a zoo and was eaten, bones and all. She shuddered. She jumped from her father's recliner and went to fix herself another sandwich. She saw that it was 10:15 and felt proud of herself. She was glad that she had a scary movie to watch; her pounding heart kept her awake.

Blanca returned to the television, and for the next three minutes watched a couple kiss beneath a palm tree. Then the sea creature came back again, and finally a flame-thrower set the creature on fire and it crawled into the sea to cool off.

Blanca turned off the television. She ate her second sandwich slowly because she was getting stuffed. She heard a firecracker and ran to look out the window. All she saw was fog glowing under the porch light. She heard

another firecracker, and next a string of firecrackers followed by a whistling rocket; then there was laughter and
the sound of a car door slamming.

"It's not twelve," she said to herself. She went into
the kitchen and looked at the clock: 10:47. She returned
to the living room and peered out the window. The
neighbors across the street, where the cherry-red Chevy
sat parked on the lawn, were having a party. They were
loud and probably drunk. At that moment a cat meowed,
and once again Blanca pressed her face to the glass, scanning her front lawn. The cat meowed again and again.

"Poor cat," she whispered. She opened the front door
and looked out. The meowing was louder, and so was
the party. Barefoot, Blanca tiptoed onto the cement porch
and called, "Here, kitty-kitty-kitty." She scanned the yard,
which was bathed in the orange glow of the porch light.
She called again, "Kitty-kitty-kitty." She was calling a
third time when a gust of wind rippled her robe and then
slammed the front door behind her.

"Oh, no," Blanca cried. She raced to the door: it was
locked. She pushed and threw her small body against the
door, crying, "Open up, you stupid thing!"

Blanca looked in the front window, her hands shading
her eyes from the porch light. She could see the mess
she'd left on her father's TV tray. "Darn it," she yelled,
startled by another firecracker. Then she ran around to
the back of the house and tried the back door. It was
locked, too, and so were the windows.

She shuddered and hugged herself. When a string of

firecrackers went off, she yelled, "Shut up." From the back door Blanca raced to her parents' bedroom, where she stood and thought about banging on the window. Her mother would throw a fit if she peeked out between the curtains and saw her daughter jumping from one foot to the other, freezing.

Blanca decided to go back to the front yard and saw a group of neighbors, beers in hand, popping firecrackers.

A man looked in her direction, and, afraid, she slid back into the shadow of the house, away from the glare of the porch light. Did he see me? she asked herself. She stood motionless for a while, and when she couldn't stand the cold any longer, she ran over to her father's tow truck. She yanked on the door handle, and it gave with a squeak. Inside the cab she found a blanket, which she wrapped around her shoulders, and folded her muddy feet under her. She rubbed her hands together, firing up a friction of warmth.

Blanca heard someone say, "Someone's messin' with Ray's truck." She stopped rubbing her hands and held her breath. The music stopped and so did the neighbors' loud noise and the firecrackers. Tears rose to Blanca's eyes. She couldn't remember ever before having cried two times in one day, but tears were flowing into her hands as she covered her face. She had thought New Year's Eve was supposed to be a happy day, but so far, with less than an hour to go, she had had a miserable time.

"What are you doing!" a man asked. A woolen hat was pulled over his ears. His goatee was thin and shaped like a dagger. A crucifix earring dangled from one ear.

"I got locked out," Blanca cried, her hands covering her face.

"Locked out? Aren't you Ray's daughter? Where's your dad?"

She blubbered about how she had wanted to go to the snow and how her father had promised to stay up to celebrate New Year's with her. She even cried about Dulce kicking the soccer ball into her face and how she had had an awful day.

The man drew Blanca into his arms and carried her into the house across the street. He placed her near the floor furnace and called, "Hey, Mom, it's Ray's daughter."

His mother shuffled into the living room, waving away the party-goers. She was dressed in a bathrobe and furry red slippers that looked like two short dogs. A cigarette dangled from her mouth.

"So who's this precious thing that Santa Claus brought?" the mother asked. She stubbed her cigarette out in an ashtray and issued a pale wafer of smoke as she bent down and touched Blanca's hair. "You're from across the street, *qué no?*"

When Blanca nodded, a tear splattered on the heater and began to sizzle. "I got locked out."

"Locked out?"

"Yeah, there was a cat crying, and I went out to see." More tears fell and sizzled on the floor furnace. Blanca couldn't finish her story, she was so miserable.

"Come on," the mother said. "No crybabies in this house." She gently prodded Blanca into the kitchen and poured her a cup of coffee. They sat at the kitchen table, looking at each other.

"My mom doesn't let me drink coffee," Blanca said, feeling better. "She says I'll stay short."

"It's New Year's Eve," the mother said. "Let your hair down. Celebrate." She laced Blanca's coffee with milk and three heaping spoonfuls of sugar.

Blanca took the coffee and blew on it. She saw that the kitchen clock said three minutes to twelve. This was certainly the latest she had ever stayed up. A firecracker exploded in the front yard.

The son with the goatee and dangling earring cha-cha-chaed into the kitchen and pulled his mother to her feet.

"Leave me alone, you gangster," she yelled playfully, but soon she was dancing in her son's arms and the couples were counting "nine, eight, seven, six, five, four, three, two, one—Happy New Year!"

Blanca drank her coffee and watched them dance to a song by Santana. The mother eventually returned to Blanca. She gave her a powdery white doughnut. "This will sweeten your life," she said, and then to her son she yelled, "Gilbert, get our little friend home!"

Gilbert bobbed into the kitchen, confetti in his hair. "*Simón, esa.*" He picked Blanca up, kicked a few of his party-going friends out of the way, and staggered out onto the porch.

"I don't know how you got locked out," Gilbert said, carrying her piggyback across the street. "Don't tell me, and I won't squeal. It's not my business."

Blanca had always wondered about her neighbor with the cherry-red Chevy. She pushed her doughnut toward his face, and he took a healthy bite. A few crumbs settled in his goatee. When they started to climb her porch steps, he said, "I'm goin' to put you down for a second. Stand on my shoes, so your feet won't freeze."

Blanca slid from his arms and onto his shoes. It was the way her father used to walk her around the house. Gilbert took out a credit card and worked it back and forth around the lock. He whistled as he worked and told Blanca, "I used to be in the locksmith business."

"You don't do that anymore?" she asked, a shudder running down her back as a blade of cold wind tousled her hair.

"Nah, I work at a rug company. I'm the guy on the forklift." A firecracker exploded on the neighbor's lawn. Gilbert looked over his shoulder and said, "I don't know how you can stand that noise. Low-class *vatos*."

The lock clicked and the door swung open. Blanca jumped from the man's shoes onto the living room carpet. It was good to be home. It was good to know her neighbor.

"Happy New Year," Gilbert whispered, feeling for crumbs in his beard. "You better throw yourself in bed, *chiquita*."

"Happy New Year," she smiled, and closed the door on a night that would never happen again.

SPANISH WORDS AND PHRASES

¿a quién?	to whom?
abuelita	grandma
ahorita	right now
asco	disgusting
¡ayúdame!	help me!
bigote	moustache
bueno	a telephone greeting
cállate	be quiet
cara	face
carnal	blood brother
carne asada	thin beef steak
chale	no way
chiquita	little one
chistosos	jokes
cholas	low-riding girls
chones	underpants
claro	of course
cómo	what
¿cómo no?	why not?
¿cómo te llamas, esa?	what's your name, girl?

Spanish Words and Phrases

compa	pal
como gatos y perros	(raining) like cats and dogs
dedica	dedication
entiendes	you understand
estoy cansada	I'm tired
de veras	truly
es mi ruca	she's my girl
es tan feo	it is so ugly
es tu hermanita	she's your little sister
esa	girl
ese	guy
esquincle	little kid
estás chiflado	you're crazy
feo	ugly
flaca	skinny girl
flaco	skinny guy
fideo	noodles
frijoles	beans
gato	cat
gente	people
gordita	fat girl
hace mucho frío	it is very cold
hombre	man
la vida	life
las noticias	the news
loca	crazy girl
mamacita	little mama
más fuerte	stronger

146

mensa	stupid girl
menso	stupid boy
mentirosas	liars
mi carnal	my blood brother
mi hombrecito	my little man
mi'ja	my daughter
mi'jo	my son
mi'ja, estoy cansada	my daughter, I'm tired
míra	look
muchacho, ven acá	boy, come here
mocoso	snotty
nada	nothing
nalgas	buttocks
nina	godmother
niña	young girl
niños	children
no sé	I don't know
ojos	eyes
órale	all right
papi	papa
pero	but
piojo	louse, flea
policía	police
por favor	please
pues	well then
pues sí	of course
qué	what
qué cochina	how dirty

¿qué dices?	what are you saying?
qué guapo	how handsome
¿qué hacen a mi familia?	what's happening to my family?
qué idea	what an idea
qué lástima	what a pity
qué loco	how crazy
¿qué no?	isn't that right?
¿qué pasa?	what's happening?
¿qué pasó?	what's happened?
¿quién sabe?	who knows?
ruca	girlfriend
señora	ma'am
simón	yes
su familia	your family
también	also
vato loco	crazy dude
vatos	guys
viejo	old man
y tú	and you
¿y tu dedica?	and your dedication?
¿y tu escuela?	and your school?

CONNECTIONS

Taking Off
Kristen Binck

Like Araceli in Soto's "Nickel-a-Pound Plane Ride," Elise experiences the thrills and chills of flight, but for different reasons: Araceli just wants to have fun, but Elise is going on a somewhat tense visit to her father's new family. Kristen Binck wrote this story when she was in her sophomore year (tenth grade) at Glenelg High School in Glenelg, Maryland.

Elise hates takeoff. The way her body gets pushed back into the seat and her ears pop. Her stomach is queasy and she gets that awful feeling, that feeling of having no control. The other passengers on the plane don't seem to notice, acting as if flying is a perfectly normal part of their daily routine. For just a moment she is filled with anger at these calm people, wishing they would panic like she always does. Elise knows she is overreacting, knows that her plane won't crash. Her mind understands fully, yet she still worries. She can't help it; she worries a lot.

Once safely in the air, Elise tries to relax. She puts on her headphones so that the woman next to her won't try to start a conversation. She doesn't feel like talking now. Leaning back in her seat, she looks out the window and thanks God that it's not cloudy. Elise feels her muscles relax, tension draining slowly out of her.

She closes her eyes and tries to imagine what it will be like in Washington. She doesn't care about the city itself, because all big cities are alike. Dirty, crowded, and loud, they are perfect for making her nervous. What Elise tries to imagine is what *they* will be like. The picture that Bobby, her brother, sent her looks like a page from a magazine. Tina, a tall, slightly awkward ten-year-old, is standing next to her mother, Beth. The two are very beautiful and look alike, with black hair, dark eyes, and shy smiles showing only a few blazing white teeth. Bobby is holding the baby, Christopher, on his shoulders. Though only half-brothers, the resemblance is

From *Merlyn's Pen: Fiction, Essays, and Poems by America's Teens.*

strong because both have their father's dark coloring. Her father stands in the middle, beaming brightly, his arms around his new family. Elise thinks about how she would look standing there. Her blond hair, blue eyes, and pale skin would make it seem as though part of the picture was underdeveloped. She is her mother's daughter.

She snaps off her headset when she hears the pilot's voice on the intercom. He announces that breakfast will soon be served. Feeling how hungry she is, Elise remembers fighting with her mother over not wanting to eat a snack that morning. Her mother had been right, as usual, and although she never says "I told you so," you can always see it in her eyes.

Mom had been very nervous this morning, pestering Elise with worries and nagging her with questions. She was afraid that Elise might get lost, or that her flight would be delayed. She asked her over and over if she had remembered everything, and if she had packed her toothbrush, and if she was sure she knew where to meet her father. Elise had been angry and yelled at her mother for bothering her, but inside she was asking herself the same questions. Despite how her mother can annoy her, Elise knows how alike they really are. Bobby told her once that her father said her mother's nagging really got to him. He said she worried too much. If he stopped loving her mother because of who she was, how then will he love Elise, the image of her mother in looks and personality? Perhaps after the month is up and she returns home for school, he will be glad to see her go.

When the breakfast cart finally reaches her row, Elise chooses a hot food tray and an orange juice. The woman next to her must have eaten this morning because she only has a cup of coffee. When she sees her food, Elise is jealous of this woman for being so smart and angry with herself for not listening to her mother. The woman must have seen her staring, because she smiles a friendly smile that Elise returns politely before turning her attention to her own meal. She finishes eating quickly, partly because she is so hungry and partly because most of the food is not edible.

After the trays have been cleared away, Elise pulls out the picture of the family again. Bobby looks so happy with them, like he really belongs there. It had been such a surprise last fall when he anounced that he wanted to leave. He had kept in close contact with their father ever since he had resurfaced and settled down five years ago. Bobby had even gone to visit when Christopher was born, but no one expected him to want to pick up and move during his senior year in high school. He had tried to explain that it was something he needed to do, and that it did not mean he didn't love them. Bobby was only five when their father left, but he had memories. Elise, who was three, has no memories and doesn't want any.

On her way to the bathroom, Elise almost trips over someone's bag. Her face is burning when she reaches the lavatory, and she worries that she will open the door on someone. Once inside, she worries that someone will open the door on her. She remembers how she had been angry with Bobby at first, but she knew that he would never hurt her or her mother on purpose. Still, although she never said so, Elise thinks that her mother felt that she had somehow failed. Her eyes looked sad for so long afterward. Maybe she's afraid that Elise will want to stay, too, but Elise knows that will never happen.

Back at her seat, Elise puts the picture away. She thinks about what Bobby has told her about them. Beth is nice, kind of quiet, and eager to make a good impression. She is an art buyer who is also interested in vegetarian foods and yoga. When Elise's mother heard this, she said that was the kind of person her father once called "artsy-fartsy." Their stepsister, Tina, rarely talks to Bobby because she is painfully shy. She spends a lot of time alone, reading. Christopher is adorable, but so are all two-year-olds when they aren't sick. Bobby thinks their father is really cool, and he always refers to him as Dad. Dad loves the city and eating out. He also has a new habit—spending lots of time with his kids. He picked that one up a little too late for Elise.

Elise has never known him as Dad. At home he is "my father" or "her father" or "your father." Her mother doesn't call him Robert because they never refer to him that specifically. Dad is someone you love, and Elise doesn't love her father. Suddenly she begins to worry about what she will call him when she gets there. Tina calls him Robert, but he wouldn't like that from his own daughter. Still, she can't bring herself to call him Dad. Maybe she can get through a month without addressing him at all.

The pilot comes on again to announce that they will begin to land soon. Elise hates landing as much as she hates taking off. Her stomach tightens and she wonders why she ever agreed to come at all. Probably because of Bobby. She missed him so much . . .

But now, as she nears National Airport, she is furious with him. She worked so hard to distance herself, to keep her father from hurting her again, and here she is on his doorstep. She won't admit, even to herself, that she wants to see them, to see what is so special about them that wasn't special about her. What made them able to tie him down when his own daughter could not.

Elise fights back a sob as the plane rushes toward the runway. She is so scared that she closes her eyes and braces herself. When she opens her eyes, the plane is on the ground, taxiing toward the airport. She had been so sure that they would crash, but they landed safely. She gathers her bags and steps off the plane, a tight knot in her stomach.

■ ■ ■

The Use of Fiction
Naomi Shihab Nye

*Although this poem is set in San Antonio, Texas, where Naomi
Shihab Nye resides, the boy in the poem easily could have been a
character in* Local News. *The main difference is that* Local News
*tells a neighborhood's story by describing characters who live in
it, whereas "The Use of Fiction" tells its story through the eyes of a
visitor to the neighborhood.*

A boy claims he saw you on a bicycle last week,
Touring his neighborhood. "West Cypress Street!" he shouts,
As if your being there and his seeing you
Were some sort of benediction.

To be alive, to be standing outside
On a tender February evening . . .
"It was a blue bicycle, ma'am, your braid was flying,
I said hello and you laughed, remember?"

You almost tell him your bicycle seat is thick with dust,
The tires have been flat for months.
But his face, that radiant flower, says you are his friend,
He has told his mother your name!
Maybe this is a clear marble
He will hide in his sock drawer for months.
So who now, in a world of figures,
Would deny West Cypress Street,
Throwing up clouds into this literal sky?
"Yes, Amigo"—hand on shoulder—
"It was I."

Beautiful As the Day

from Five Children and It

Edith Nesbit

The children in this excerpt, like those in Local News, *are restless, curious, and frequently unsupervised, and they get into trouble all too easily, with unpredictable consequences. The main difference, though, is that Soto's world is that of modern California, whereas the world of Edith Nesbit (1858–1924) is that of middle-class England at the end of the nineteenth century.*

The White House was on the edge of a hill, with a wood behind it and the chalk-quarry on one side and the gravel-pit on the other. Down at the bottom of the hill was a level plain, with queer-shaped white buildings where people burnt lime, and a big red brewery and other houses; and when the big chimneys were smoking and the sun was setting, the valley looked as if it was filled with golden mist, and the limekilns and oast-houses[1] glimmered and glittered till they were like an enchanted city out of the Arabian Nights.

. . . Grown-up people find it very difficult to believe really wonderful things, unless they have what they call proof. But children will believe almost anything, and grown-ups know this. That is why they tell you that the earth is round like an orange, when you can see perfectly well that it is flat and lumpy; and why they say that the earth goes round the sun, when you can see for yourself any day that the sun gets up in the morning and goes to bed at night like a good sun as it is, and the earth knows its place, and lies as still as a mouse. Yet I daresay you believe all that about the earth and the sun, and if so you will find it quite easy to believe that before Anthea and Cyril and the others had been a week in the

---

1. Kilns in which hops and barley are dried.

country they had found a fairy. At least they called it that, because that was what it called itself; and of course it knew best, but it was not at all like any fairy you ever saw or heard of or read about.

It was at the gravel-pits. Father had to go away suddenly on business, and mother had gone away to stay with Granny, who was not very well. They both went in a great hurry, and when they were gone the house seemed dreadfully quiet and empty, and the children wandered from one room to another and looked at the bits of paper and string on the floors left over from the packing, and not yet cleared up, and wished they had something to do. It was Cyril who said:

'I say, let's take our Margate spades and go and dig in the gravel-pits. We can pretend it's seaside.'

'Father said it was once,' Anthea said; 'he says there are shells there thousands of years old.'

So they went. Of course they had been to the edge of the gravel-pit and looked over, but they had not gone down into it for fear father should say they mustn't play there, and the same with the chalk-quarry. The gravel-pit is not really dangerous if you don't try to climb down the edges, but go the slow safe way round by the road, as if you were a cart.

Each of the children carried its own spade, and took it in turns to carry the Lamb. He was the baby, and they called him that because 'Baa' was the first thing he ever said. They called Anthea 'Panther', which seems silly when you read it, but when you say it it sounds a little like her name.

The gravel-pit is very large and wide, with grass growing round the edges at the top, and dry stringy wildflowers, purple and yellow. It is like a giant's wash-hand basin. And there are mounds of gravel, and holes in the sides of the basin where gravel has been taken out, and high up in the steep sides there are the little holes that are the little front doors of the little sand-martins' little houses.

The children built a castle, of course, but castle-building is rather poor fun when you have no hope of the swishing tide ever coming in to fill up the moat and wash away the draw-bridge, and, at the happy last, to wet everybody up to the waist at least.

Cyril wanted to dig out a cave to play smugglers in, but the others thought it might bury them alive, so it ended in all spades going to work to dig a hole through the castle to Australia. These children, you see, believed that the world was round, and that on the other side the little Australian boys and girls were really walking wrong way up, like flies on the ceiling, with their heads hanging down into the air.

The children dug and they dug and they dug, and their hands got sandy and hot and red, and their faces got damp and shiny. The Lamb had tried to eat the sand, and had cried so hard when he found that it was not, as he had supposed, brown sugar, that he was now tired out, and was lying asleep in a warm fat bunch in the middle of the half-finished castle. This left his brothers and sisters free to work really hard, and the hole that was to come out in Australia soon grew so deep that Jane . . . begged the others to stop.

'Suppose the bottom of the hole gave way suddenly,' she said, 'and you tumbled out among the little Australians, all the sand would get in their eyes.'

'Yes,' said Robert; 'and they would hate us, and throw stones at us, and not let us see the kangaroos, or opossums, or blue-gums, or Emu Brand birds, or anything.'

Cyril and Anthea knew that Australia was not quite so near as all that, but they agreed to stop using the spades and go on with their hands. This was quite easy, because the sand at the bottom of the hole was very soft and fine and dry, like sea-sand. And there were little shells in it.

. . .

'How did the sea get carried away?' Robert asked.

'Not in a pail, silly,' said his brother. 'Father says the earth got too hot underneath, like you do in bed sometimes, so it just hunched up its shoulders, and the sea had to slip off, like the blankets do off us, and the shoulder was left sticking out, and turned into dry land. Let's go and look for shells; I think that little cave looks likely, and I see something sticking out there like a bit of wrecked ship's anchor, and it's beastly hot in the Australian hole.'

The others agreed, but Anthea went on digging. She always liked to finish a thing when she had once begun it. She felt it would be a disgrace to leave that hole without getting through to Australia.

The cave was disappointing, because there were no shells, and the wrecked ship's anchor turned out to be only the broken end of a pickaxe handle, and the cave party were just making up their minds that the sand makes you thirstier when it is not by the seaside, and someone had suggested going home for lemonade, when Anthea suddenly screamed:

'Cyril! Come here! Oh, come quick! It's alive! It'll get away! Quick!'

They all hurried back.

'It's a rat . . .,' said Robert. 'Father says they infest old places—and this must be pretty old if the sea was here thousands of years ago.'

'Perhaps it is a snake,' said Jane, shuddering.

'Let's look,' said Cyril, jumping into the hole. 'I'm not afraid of snakes. I like them. If it is a snake I'll tame it, and it will follow me everywhere, and I'll let it sleep round my neck at night.'

'No, you won't,' said Robert firmly. He shared Cyril's bedroom. 'But you may if it's a rat.'

'Oh, don't be silly!' said Anthea; 'it's not a rat, it's much bigger. And it's not a snake. It's got feet; I saw them; and fur! No—not the spade. You'll hurt it! Dig with your hands.'

'And let it hurt me instead! That's so likely, isn't it?' said
Cyril, seizing a spade.

'Oh, don't!' said Anthea. 'Squirrel, don't. I—it sounds
silly, but it said something. It really and truly did.'

'What?'

'It said, "You let me alone".'

But Cyril merely observed that his sister must have gone
off her nut, and he and Robert dug with spades while Anthea
sat on the edge of the hole, jumping up and down with hotness
and anxiety. They dug carefully, and presently everyone could
see that there really was something moving in the bottom of the
Australian hole.

Then Anthea cried out, 'I'M not afraid. Let me dig,' and
fell on her knees and began to scratch like a dog does when he
has suddenly remembered where it was that he buried his bone.

'Oh, I felt fur,' she cried, half laughing and half crying. 'I
did indeed! I did!' when suddenly a dry husky voice in the sand
made them all jump back, and their hearts jumped nearly as
fast as they did.

'Let me alone,' it said. And now everyone heard the voice
and looked at the others to see if they had too.

'But we want to see you,' said Robert bravely.

'I wish you'd come out,' said Anthea, also taking courage.

'Oh, well—if that's your wish,' the voice said, and the sand
stirred and spun and scattered, and something brown and furry
and fat came rolling out into the hole and the sand fell off it,
and it sat there yawning and rubbing the ends of its eyes with
its hands.

'I believe I must have dropped asleep,' it said, stretching
itself.

The children stood round the hole in a ring, looking at the
creature they had found. It was worth looking at. Its eyes were
on long horns like a snail's eyes, and it could move them in and
out like telescopes; it had ears like a bat's ears, and its tubby

body was shaped like a spider's and covered with thick soft fur; its legs and arms were furry too, and it had hands and feet like a monkey's.

'What on earth is it?' Jane said. 'Shall we take it home?'

The thing turned its long eyes to look at her, and said: 'Does she always talk nonsense, or is it only the rubbish on her head that makes her silly?'

It looked scornfully at Jane's hat as it spoke.

'She doesn't mean to be silly,' Anthea said gently; 'we none of us do, whatever you may think! Don't be frightened; we don't want to hurt you, you know.'

'Hurt me!' it said. 'Me frightened? Upon my word! Why, you talk as if I were nobody in particular.' All its fur stood out like a cat's when it is going to fight.

'Well,' said Anthea, still kindly, 'perhaps if we knew who you are in particular we could think of something to say that wouldn't make you cross. Everything we've said so far seems to have. Who are you? And don't get angry! Because really we don't know.'

'You don't know?' it said. 'Well, I knew the world had changed—but—well, really—do you mean to tell me seriously you don't know a Psammead when you see one?'

'A Sammyadd? That's Greek to me.'

'So it is to everyone,' said the creature sharply. 'Well, in plain English, then, a sand-fairy. Don't you know a Sand-fairy when you see one?'

It looked so grieved and hurt that Jane hastened to say, 'Of course I see you are, now. It's quite plain now one comes to look at you.'

'You came to look at me, several sentences ago,' it said crossly, beginning to curl up again in the sand.

'Oh—don't go away again! Do talk some more,' Robert cried. 'I didn't know you were a Sand-fairy, but I knew directly I saw you that you were much the wonderfullest thing I'd ever seen.'

The Sand-fairy seemed a shade less disagreeable after this.

'It isn't talking I mind,' it said, 'as long as you're reasonably civil. But I'm not going to make polite conversation for you. If you talk nicely to me, perhaps I'll answer you, and perhaps I won't. Now say something.'

Of course no one could think of anything to say, but at last Robert thought of 'How long have you lived here?' and he said it at once.

'Oh, ages—several thousand years,' replied the Psammead.

'Tell us all about it. Do.'

. . .

It is wonderful how quickly you get used to things, even the most astonishing. Five minutes before, the children had had no more idea than you that there was such a thing as a sand-fairy in the world, and now they were talking to it as though they had known it all their lives. It drew its eyes in and said:

'How very sunny it is—quite like old times. Where do you get your Megatheriums from now?'

'What?' said the children all at once. It is very difficult always to remember that 'what' is not polite, especially in moments of surprise or agitation.

'Are Pterodactyls plentiful now?' the Sand-fairy went on.

The children were unable to reply.

'What do you have for breakfast?' the Fairy said impatiently, 'and who gives it you?'

'Eggs and bacon, and bread-and-milk, and porridge and things. Mother gives it us. What are Mega-what's-its-names and Ptero-what-do-you-call-thems? And does anyone have them for breakfast?'

'Why, almost everyone had Pterodactyl for breakfast in my time! Pterodactyls were something like crocodiles and something like birds—I believe they were very good grilled. You see it was like this: of course there were heaps of sand-fairies then, and in the morning early you went out and hunted for them, and when you'd found one it gave you your wish. People used to send their little boys down to the seashore early in the morning before breakfast to get the day's wishes, and very often the eldest boy in the family would be told to wish for a Megatherium, ready jointed for cooking. It was as big as an elephant, you see, so there was a good deal of meat on it. And if they wanted fish, the Ichthyosaurus was asked for—he was twenty to forty feet long, so there was plenty of him. And for poultry there was the Plesiosaurus; there were nice pickings on that too. Then the other children could wish for other things. But when people had dinner-parties it was nearly always Megatheriums; and Ichthyosaurus, because his fins were a great delicacy and his tail made soup.'

'There must have been heaps and heaps of cold meat left over,' said Anthea, who meant to be a good housekeeper some day.

'Oh no,' said the Psammead, 'that would never have done. Why, of course at sunset what was left over turned into stone. You find the stone bones of the Megatherium and things all over the place even now, they tell me.'

'Who tell you?' asked Cyril; but the Sand-fairy frowned and began to dig very fast with its furry hands.

'Oh, don't go!' they all cried; 'tell us more about it when it was Megatheriums for breakfast! Was the world like this then?'

It stopped digging.

'Not a bit,' it said; 'it was nearly all sand where I lived, and coal grew on trees, and the periwinkles were as big as tea-trays —you find them now; they're turned into stone. . . .'

'But why did you stop living in the castles?' asked Robert.

'It's a sad story,' said the Psammead gloomily. 'It was because . . . the nasty wet bubbling sea used to come in, and of course as soon as a sand-fairy got wet it caught cold, and generally died. And so there got to be fewer and fewer, and, whenever you found a fairy and had a wish, you used to wish for a

Megatherium, and eat twice as much as you wanted, because it might be weeks before you got another wish.'

'And did you get wet?' Robert inquired.

The Sand-fairy shuddered. 'Only once,' it said; 'the end of the twelfth hair of my top left whisker—I feel the place still in damp weather. It was only once, but it was quite enough for me. I went away as soon as the sun had dried my poor dear whisker. I scurried away to the back of the beach, and dug myself a house deep in warm dry sand, and there I've been ever since. And the sea changed its lodgings afterwards. And now I'm not going to tell you another thing.'

'Just one more, please,' said the children. 'Can you give wishes now?'

'Of course,' said it; 'didn't I give you yours a few minutes ago? You said, "I wish you'd come out," and I did.'

'Oh, please, [ca]n't we have another?'

'Yes, but be quick about it. I'm tired of you.'

I daresay you have often thought what you would do if you had three wishes given you. . . . These children had often talked this matter over, but, now [that] the chance had suddenly come to them, they could not make up their minds.

'Quick,' said the Sand-fairy crossly. No one could think of anything, only Anthea did manage to remember a private wish of her own and Jane's which they had never told the boys. She knew the boys would not care about it—but still it was better than nothing.

'I wish we were all as beautiful as the day,' she said in a great hurry.

The children looked at each other, but each could see that the others were not any better-looking than usual. The Psammead pushed out its long eyes, and seemed to be holding its breath and swelling itself out till it was twice as fat and furry as before. Suddenly it let its breath go in a long sigh.

'I'm really afraid I can't manage it,' it said apologetically; 'I must be out of practice.'

The children were horribly disappointed.

'Oh, do try again!' they said.

'Well,' said the Sand-fairy, 'the fact is, I was keeping back a little strength to give the rest of you your wishes with. If you'll be contented with one wish a day [among] the lot of you I daresay I can [do] it. Do you agree to that?'

'Yes, oh yes!' said Jane and Anthea. The boys nodded. They did not believe the Sand-fairy could do it. . . .

It stretched out its eyes farther than ever, and swelled and swelled and swelled.

'I do hope it won't hurt itself,' said Anthea.

'Or crack its skin,' Robert said anxiously.

Everyone was very much relieved when the Sand-fairy, after getting so big that it almost filled up the hole in the sand, suddenly let out its breath and went back to its proper size.

'That's all right,' it said, panting heavily. 'It'll come easier to-morrow.'

'Did it hurt much?' asked Anthea.

'Only my poor whisker, thank you,' said he, 'but you're a kind and thoughtful child. Good day.'

It scratched suddenly and fiercely with its hands and feet, and disappeared in the sand. Then the children looked at each other, and each child suddenly found itself alone with three perfect strangers, all radiantly beautiful.

. . . Anthea spoke first—

'Excuse me,' she said very politely to Jane, who now had enormous blue eyes and a cloud of russet hair, 'but have you seen two little boys and a little girl anywhere about?'

'I was just going to ask you that,' said Jane. And then Cyril cried:

'Why, it's you! I know the hole in your pinafore! You ARE Jane, aren't you? And you're the Panther; I can see your dirty handkerchief that you forgot to change after you'd cut your thumb! Crikey! The wish has come off, after all. I say, am I as handsome as you are?'

'If you're Cyril, I liked you much better as you were before,' said Anthea decidedly. . . .

'You two girls are like Christmas cards, then—that's all—silly Christmas cards,' said Robert angrily. . . .

'Well, it's no use finding fault with each other,' said Anthea; 'let's get the Lamb and lug it home to dinner. The servants will admire us most awfully, you'll see.'

Baby was just waking when they got to him, and not one of the children but was relieved to find that he at least was not as beautiful as the day, but just the same as usual.

'I suppose he's too young to have wishes naturally,' said Jane. 'We shall have to mention him specially next time.'

Anthea ran forward and held out her arms.

'Come to own Panther, ducky,' she said.

The Baby looked at her disapprovingly, and put a sandy pink thumb in his mouth, Anthea was his favourite sister.

'Come then,' she said.

. . .

'Wants my Panty,' said the Lamb dismally, and his lip trembled.

'Here, come on, Veteran,' said Robert, 'come and have a yidey on Yobby's back.'

'Yah, narky narky boy,' howled the Baby, giving way altogether. Then the children knew the worst. The baby did not know them! They looked at each other in despair, and it was terrible to each, in this dire emergency, to meet only the beautiful eyes of perfect strangers, instead of the merry, friendly, commonplace, twinkling, jolly little eyes of its own brothers and sisters.

'This is most truly awful,' said Cyril when he had tried to lift up the Lamb, and the Lamb had scratched like a cat and bellowed like a bull. 'We've got to make friends with him! I can't carry him home screaming like that. Fancy having to make friends with our own baby!—it's too silly.'

That, however, was exactly what they had to do. It took over an hour, and the task was not rendered any easier by the fact that the Lamb was by this time as hungry as a lion and as thirsty as a desert. At last he consented to allow these strangers to carry him home by turns, but as he refused to hold on to such new acquaintances he was a dead weight and most exhausting.

'Thank goodness, we're home!' said Jane, staggering through the iron gate to where Martha, the nursemaid, stood at the front door shading her eyes with her hand and looking out anxiously. 'Here! Do take Baby!'

Martha snatched the Baby from her arms.

'Thanks be, he's safe back,' she said. 'Where are the others, and whoever to goodness gracious are all of you?'

'We're us, of course,' said Robert.

'And who's us, when you're at home?' asked Martha scornfully.

'I tell you it's us, only we're beautiful as the day,' said Cyril. 'I'm Cyril, and these are the others, and we're jolly hungry. Let us in, and don't be a silly idiot.'

Martha merely dratted Cyril's impudence and tried to shut the door in his face.

'I know we look different, but I'm Anthea, and we're so tired, and it's long past dinner-time.'

'Then go home to your dinners, whoever you are; and if our children put you up to this playacting you can tell them from me they'll catch it, so they know what to expect!' With that she did bang the door. Cyril rang the bell violently. No answer.

Presently cook put her head out of a bedroom window and said:

'If you don't take yourselves off, and that precious sharp, I'll go and fetch the police.' And she slammed down the window.

'It's no good,' said Anthea. 'Oh, do, do come away before we get sent to prison!'

The boys said it was nonsense, and the law of England couldn't put you in prison for just being as beautiful as the day, but all the same they followed the others out into the lane.

'We shall be our proper selves after sunset, I suppose,' said Jane. . . .

'Oh,' cried Anthea suddenly, 'perhaps we shall turn into stone at sunset, like the Megatheriums did, so that there m[ight no]t be any of us left over for the next day.'

She began to cry, so did Jane. Even the boys turned pale. No one had the heart to say anything. It was a horrible after-noon. There was no house near where the children could beg a crust of bread or even a glass of water. They were afraid to go to the village, because they had seen Martha go down there with a basket, and there was a local constable. True, they were all as beautiful as the day, but that is a poor comfort when you are as hungry as a hunter and as thirsty as a sponge.

Three times they tried in vain to get the servants in the White House to let them in and listen to their tale. And then Robert went alone, hoping to be able to climb in at one of the back windows and so open the door to the others. But all the windows were out of reach, and Martha emptied a toilet-jug of cold water over him from a top window. . .

It came at last to their sitting down in a row under the hedge, with their feet in a dry ditch, waiting for sunset, and wondering whether, when the sun did set, they would turn into stone, or only into their own old natural selves; and each of them still felt lonely and among strangers, and tried not to look at the others, for, though their voices were their own, their faces were so radiantly beautiful as to be quite irritating to look at.

'I don't believe we shall turn to stone,' said Robert, breaking a long miserable silence, 'because the Sand-fairy said he'd
give us another wish to-morrow, and he couldn't if we were
stone, could he?'

The others said 'No,' but they weren't at all comforted.

. . .

The . . . [most miserable] silence of all was broken by Jane.
She said: 'If we DO come out of this all right, we'll ask the
Sammyadd to make it so that [people] don't notice anything
different, no matter what wishes we have.'

The others only grunted. They were too wretched even to
make good resolutions.

At last hunger and fright and crossness[2] and tiredness—four
very nasty things—all joined together to bring one nice thing,
and that was sleep. The children lay asleep in a row, with their
beautiful eyes shut and their beautiful mouths open. Anthea
woke first. The sun had set, and the twilight was coming on.

Anthea pinched herself very hard, to make sure, and when
she found she could still feel pinching she decided that she
was not stone, and then she pinched the others. They, also,
were soft.

'Wake up,' she said, almost in tears of joy; 'it's all right,
we're not stone. And oh, Cyril, how nice and ugly you do look,
with your old freckles and your brown hair and your little eyes.
And so do you all!' she added, so that they might not feel
jealous.

When they got home they were very much scolded by
Martha, who told them about the strange children.

'A good-looking lot, I must say, but that impudent.'

'I know,' said Robert, who knew by experience how hopeless it would be to try to explain things to Martha.

'And where on earth have you been all this time, you
naughty little things, you?'

---

2. Anger.

'In the lane.'

'Why didn't you come home hours ago?'

'We couldn't because of them,' said Anthea.

'Who?'

'The children who were as beautiful as the day. They kept us there till after sunset. We couldn't come back till they'd gone. You don't know how we hated them! Oh, do, do give us some supper—we are so hungry.'

'Hungry! I should think so,' said Martha angrily; 'out all day like this. Well, I hope it'll be a lesson to you not to go picking up with strange children—down here after measles, as likely as not! Now mind, if you see them again, don't you speak to them—not one word nor so much as a look—but come straight away and tell me. I'll spoil their beauty for them!'

'If ever we do see them again we'll tell you,' Anthea said; and Robert, fixing his eyes fondly on the cold beef that was being brought in on a tray by cook, added in heartfelt undertones—'And we'll take jolly good care we never do see them again.'

And they never have.

■ ■ ■

Through Anger and Love
Toshio Mori

Like Alex in the Local News *story "First Job," the Japanese American
boy in this story, Haruo, is looking for a way to make money. Like
Alex, he lives in California, but unlike* Local News, *this story shows
what life was like during the 1930s. Toshio Mori (1910–1980) was
himself born in California.*

From a parked automobile Haruo stuck his head out a little and
peered across the street. Yes, he was still standing by the entrance
talking to several men. His old man was talking and laughing as if
nothing had happened yesterday. Had he forgotten already? No,
his old man couldn't forget that easily. Haruo cautiously drew
back and sat on the fender. Five minutes to seven by the City Hall
clock. Promptly at seven, he knew, the flower market was going
to open. What should he buy? What flowers were most popular,
and most profitable? Suddenly he heard footsteps approaching
the car. Instantly he was on his feet, and without looking back
scurried around the corner. Safely past the corner he increased his
pace. At a hundred yards he began to puff with exertion and
slackened a bit. Just ahead he spied an alley and ran for it. Puffing
and coughing he rested his nine-year-old body, his eyes trained
on the sidewalk. Two minutes passed and nobody came after
him. Slowly he came out and looked down the street and sighed
with relief.

The market was open by now. Well, let the others go in first.
He would walk around the block and take his time. Unhurriedly
he stopped and looked at the store windows. Every now and
then he looked up and down the street. Watching his chance
he would slip in the market and make his purchase. He must
look out for his old man. Then he must act natural when buying
from the wholesalers so they would think that he was buying for
his old man. Several minutes ago he was unsure of himself. He
couldn't believe that he would be able to go through with it.

Now he was sure of himself. He knew what flowers to get and
where to get it from. His father bought a lot of things from
Matsumoto and Toscana. Matsumoto was a grower of
carnations and Toscana raised roses. They knew him well.
It would be easy. If only his old man would not appear at
the wrong time.

Nearing the market once more Haruo slowed down. His eyes
darted from the market entrance to the adjoining wholesale stores.
Cautiously he stepped behind the row of parked cars watching for
his father. He was not in sight. Should he take a chance now or
wait awhile? He watched a number of people coming in and out
of the market. Flower business must have been good yesterday.
Almost all the florists were present. Should he hurry and buy
before the flowers were all gone? Several more florists came out
with armfuls of flowers. Haruo became desperate. He hurriedly
crossed the street to a spot near the entrance. Growing bolder he
peered through the window, watching all sides, and then he saw
his father.

His father was in the rear of the market purchasing cyclamen
and mixed plants. He looked very much absorbed in the plants.
Should he slip in now? Haruo could see Matsumoto, whose table
was near the entrance. At least he could get the carnations. Wait
a minute. He became suspicious, cautious. Was his old man pur-
posely in the rear so he would fall in a trap? Maybe his old man
had seen him a few minutes ago and asked Matsumoto to look
out for him. That would be terrible. Then he would have to go
back home crawling on his knees. Undoubtedly his father would
further humiliate him and kick him out of the house. Maybe
Matsumoto did not know. He looked keenly at the carnation
grower's face, watching for a tell-tale sign that he was looking
out for his old man. No, he did not know. Matsumoto's face was
calm and relaxed. His eyes did not shift about. Then he looked
in the rear of the market watching for his old man. He was not
around. He was gone. Eagerly he walked in heading straight for
Matsumoto's table.

Haruo's face fell. Matsumoto's table was bare. Where did his flowers go? Did he sell out? He hesitated in his tracks. Matsumoto's eyes brightened.

"Hello, Haruo!" he cried. "How are you? My, you've grown. And how is your mother?"

"Fine," Haruo said hurriedly. He looked over the table. "Did you sell out? Have you any carnations left?"

"Do you want carnations?" Matsumoto asked. "Let's see. How many do you want?"

"Ten bunches," Haruo said eagerly.

The man looked under the table and started unwrapping a big bundle. "All right, Haruo," he said. "I'll give you ten. Mixed colors?"

"Yes, but give me lots of red."

Matsumoto laughed heartily and his belly shook. "You're a smart boy, Haruo. You know what sells."

Haruo looked about. Matsumoto laughed and talked too loud. He must get away. "Will you please wrap it up?"

"Are you going to take it with you now or is your father coming to pick it up?" he asked.

"I want it now," Haruo said quickly.

Matsumoto hummed a tune and took his time wrapping. Finally he handed over the package. "All right, Haruo."

"How much is it?" Haruo asked.

"Dollar and a half. I'm charging you only fifteen cents a bunch."

"Pay you next time," Haruo said.

"Sure. That's all right," Matsumoto cried, waving his hand.

Haruo fairly ran to Toscana's table. He must hurry. His father might return any minute. His eyes brightened at the sight of Toscana's good roses piled high on his table.

"Hello, boy," called the Italian. "Do you want to buy nice roses? I'll give you a bargain today."

Haruo picked up a bunch to see if the outer petals of the roses were bruised, and then satisfied examined the bases of the

stems for the telltale mark of old flowers. Toscana chuckled and
picked up several bunches for Haruo to examine.

"All fresh flowers, my boy. No kidding," he said. "You want to
buy for your papa?"

"How much?" Haruo asked hurriedly.

Toscana counted off six bunches. "Two dollars to you. A real
bargain."

"I'll take it," he said quickly.

Haruo looked about while he waited for the man to finish
wrapping. He must get away. Any minute now his old man would
be coming back. Which entrance should he take, the front or the
rear? Eagerly he accepted the package from Toscana.

"All right, boy," the nurseryman said, nodding and smiling.

With both arms loaded with packages Haruo walked off
excitedly. He must hurry. He must catch a bus and ride back to
his district and start selling his flowers. He quickened his little
strides in the direction of the rear entrance. Suddenly from the
front entrance came a familiar cry. "Haruo! Come back! Haruo!"

Terror-stricken he broke for the rear door. Gripping his bun-
dles tight to his sides he ran past several tables unheeding the
cries. Reaching the sidewalk he cut sharply to his right and then
across the street. He must not be caught. It would be the end of
him. He must get away. Running swiftly around the corner he
headed for Seventh. He must shake his father off his trail. Should
he go up or down Seventh? He must go up to reach the bus line,
but suppose his old man was waiting for him at the next block?
No, that wouldn't do. Should he run straight for First and wait
around the pier, and later retrace his steps? That would be loss of
time. No, he must go down Seventh and walk back to Twelfth.
Then he remembered the jitney running on Seventh and his eyes
brightened. His father would never think of the jitney.

To make sure his old man was not following, Haruo ran a
couple of blocks more and headed for Sixth. At the corner of Sixth
he sat puffing on the gutter looking in all directions, expecting the
appearance of his father. Anxiously he looked to see if the flowers

were bruised and the stems broken. They looked all right, and his anxiety turned to relief. He must sell them before noon while in good condition. In the afternoon they would start wilting without water.

Five minutes went by and his father did not appear. Cautiously he walked back to Seventh and waited for the jitney. Time after time he hid among the buildings whenever a figure appeared on the street. When the jitney came he boarded quickly and asked for a transfer. He slid low in his seat so he would not be noticed from the street. Several times the driver stopped the car for passengers. Haruo held his breath at every stop, expecting his father to jump aboard. At Clay the jitney turned left and passed Eighth, Ninth, and Tenth. He noticed the tall buildings coming into view. Three more blocks and he must get off and catch his bus. Maybe he should get off a block away and make sure his old man wasn't waiting at the spot. Scrambling to his feet he asked the driver to stop at the next corner.

No sight of his old man. He walked eagerly to the corner of Thirteenth and Clay for his bus. He wished the bus would hurry. Several minutes of waiting brought restlessness and uneasiness. Was the bus never coming? Then he caught sight of it in the distance. At last!

Safely on the bus and bound for his district Haruo leaned back with relief. His father would never find him now. With his feet on the front seat Haruo braced himself. His shoes did not reach the floor. Every now and then he looked into the packages to see if the flowers were all right. A dollar and a half to Matsumoto and two dollars to Toscana. He must pay them next time. He must sell pretty near all his flowers to make a good profit. He had ten bunches of carnations and six bunches of roses. That would mean twenty dozen carnations and twelve dozen roses. He must sell cheaper than his old man. How much should he charge? Twenty-five cents a dozen for carnations and thirty-five cents a dozen for roses would be a bargain. Anybody would buy at that price. First, he would go to the shops in the district that knew him. Mazzini, the Browns, Nick, Hamilton Hardware, Rosloff Service Station, Riley, Joe, and the rest. They were friends of his old man. They would be glad to see him.

Haruo took out his pencil and pad and figured. The car moved and vibrated. Several times the flowers started to slip off the seat. Twenty dozens at twenty-five cents a dozen would be five dollars. Twelve dozen roses at thirty-five would amount to four dollars. Nine dollars for the day! That would be swell. He would give his uncle fifty cents a day for room and board.

The bus stopped and lurched. Haruo looked out of the window. Pretty soon he must get off. He put his pencil and pad in his pocket. He had better start selling right away. He must make good today. If he failed and had to go back begging for forgiveness his old man would laugh at him and give him a stick. No, he couldn't fail. When a boy has run away from home for good he should not think of going home. Even if it killed him he shouldn't. He should move on and take the consequences.

Gripping the packages tightly he waited for his block. Familiar buildings came into view. The Woolworth, Safeway, Gibson Drug, Palace Theater, Texaco Station, and Bank of America. His eyes brightened and he eagerly went forward to be let off. He could see Rosloff gingerly wiping a customer's windshield. He could see that the Browns were doing a good business. He smiled. His hometown.

Haruo got off at the next corner. For a moment he stood bewildered and hesitating. What was his plan? Where should he go first? Again the dread of uncertainty and the fear of his future shook his nerve. Did he do right by leaving home? Was he at fault and not Father? How did the quarrel begin? His cheeks burned at the thought of it. Last night his father slapped him in the face in front of his brothers and sisters and called him a fool. His brothers laughed and his sisters looked with astonishment. They saw him crying, and the hard shaking he got in addition. What did he do? He had done nothing. What was it? He didn't know. The quarrel began a long time ago. He must be bad, or his old man mistaken?

Was it his quick temper or his father's? He leaned against the telephone pole wondering what to do. Suppose the folks did not want to buy flowers today? Suppose he couldn't sell enough to pay back Matsumoto and Toscana? He would be in a fix. He couldn't live at his uncle's any length of time without paying room and board. Then he heard Rosloff's familiar voice calling, "Hello there, sonny! Come over here!"

Haruo eagerly ran across the street, his packages dangling. "How are you, Haruo?" asked the service station man. "What you got there?"

"Flowers," Haruo said eagerly. "Carnations and roses. Would you like to buy some, Mr. Rosloff?"

He laid the packages on the ground and quickly unwrapped one of them. He held a bunch of carnations in each hand. "They're nice and fresh, and a bargain. Twenty-five cents a dozen."

The man laughed. "Come inside of the station," he said. "You don't want the sun on your flowers."

Inside his cool office Rosloff picked up red and white carnation bunches. "These are swell flowers."

Haruo nodded his head. He was busy unwrapping the other bundle. "I have some nice roses too. They're thirty-five a dozen."

"Are these your dad's or your own?" the man asked.

"They're my flowers. I'm selling them," Haruo replied.

"Your dad was here five minutes ago," Rosloff said.

Haruo looked quickly at his friend. He could not tell what the man meant by it. He kept still, busying himself with the flowers.

"I'll take a dozen of pink roses and a dozen each of red and white carnations," the man said. "I'm going to take them home and surprise my wife."

"Gee, thanks!" Haruo's eyes danced as he cut the strings of the bunches and started counting.

The man took a seat and examined a headlight globe. "You cut school today, Haruo?" he asked casually.

Haruo did not look up. He kept counting the flowers slowly. "Yes, I was busy this morning."

"You should be busy in school," Rosloff quietly said. "Let your father sell flowers and worry about money."

"I can't."

"Why?" The man carefully laid the globe on the shelf.

Haruo handed over the carnations and the roses to Rosloff. Hurriedly he wrapped his remaining flowers. "I can't tell you, Mr. Rosloff."

"Did you have a fight with your dad?"

Haruo nodded his head.

"Pshaw! That's all right, son. Forget it," Rosloff said. "Sometimes you've got to taste vinegar, and sometimes honey. That's the way it goes, Haruo, whether you're young or old."

He stood shifting his weight from one foot to the other.

"Oh, I forgot, Haruo. How much do you want?"

"Eighty-five cents," Haruo said.

The man opened the register and counted the money.

"Mr. Rosloff, please don't tell my father I was here," Haruo begged. "I've run away from home."

"I won't squeal on you," the man said. "You can depend on me."

Outside Haruo stepped along gingerly, his coins jingling in the pants pocket. Eighty-five cents to the good. A swell start. With luck he might make nine dollars. He hummed a tune. He'll show his father. This was his world. Why had he been afraid several minutes ago? He knew flowers. He liked flowers. Where did his fear come from? He laughed and wondered where to try next. Up ahead the Browns' two shops bustled with activity. Miss Brown's stationery shop always had customers. She was nice to everybody. He would go in there next. Maybe her father who ran a cigar-stand next door would also buy flowers.

Haruo walked in and found a lot of customers at the counters. Almost instantly he was the center of attraction. He smiled gratefully to Miss Brown who ordered him to open the packages. People cluttered about him. A lady wanted a dozen mixed carnations. One old gentleman bought two dozen roses. A young girl took a dozen carnations for her mother. Miss Brown purchased two dozen roses, and finally escorted him to her father's place. "Dad, why don't you buy some beautiful roses for mother?" she said. "He has some of the nicest colors."

Her father looked up from his work and examined the roses. He bought two dozens. Haruo walked away, his head high in the air. He chuckled and hummed. Flushed with confidence he went in Mazzini's, Hamilton Hardware, Riley's and Joe's Garage right after another. When he came out of Joe's his packages were light. Four bunches of carnations and three bunches of roses left. His two pockets were bulging with small coins. How much had he made? He laughed. He must count the money. This was fun. Tomorrow he would take another portion of the town and keep rotating his route. He could go on forever. He smiled happily.

Haruo ran across the street into the park and sat under the shade of a tree. First, he tackled one pocketful of money and then the other. Three dollars and forty cents plus three dollars and sixty cents equals seven dollars. Seven dollars! He must have sold many dozens. Yes, sixteen dozen carnations and nine dozen roses. He could easily make nine dollars. He looked across the street at the bank clock. It was almost noon. His stomach felt empty. Nick's Cafe stood invitingly at the corner. Should he go in now and eat? He looked at the remaining carnations and roses. They were in pretty good condition. Yes, he could go in Nick's and eat and sell his flowers at the same time. He dumped his money in his pockets and picked up the flowers.

His hands bumped against the bulging pockets as he walked, and his thoughts returned to his triumph. Nine dollars gross profit minus three dollars and fifty cents cost equals five dollars and fifty cents net profit. He could do it. It meant freedom and pride. He could do as he pleased. On the way to Nick's he stopped short in front of a maroon Ford DeLuxe. It looked familiar. There was no one in it and he looked closely at the license plate. Quickly his eyes darted about the stores expecting to see his old man. His easy, springy stride of a moment ago became short hesitant steps.

Somewhere in town his father was making his rounds. Where could he be? Suppose his father caught him by surprise? A look of terror crossed his face. He must get rid of his flowers right away and slip away from the district. Every few yards Haruo looked across the street and behind him expecting his father to jump out of hiding. Hurriedly he looked in Nick's. His father wasn't there. He felt hungry, he swallowed his saliva. He could go for three hamburger sandwiches, a pie, and a glass of milk. Cautiously Haruo stood at the corner and peered inside Nick's to make sure his father wasn't among the customers. Satisfied he crossed the street for Nick's.

At the doorway Haruo hesitated. Was he taking a chance? Suppose his father should come in while he was eating and grab ahold of him? His father would surely explode and soundly spank him in front of Nick and everybody. No, he mustn't take such a risk. First, he would go around the block and see if his father was in any of the stores. Then he would hurry back, order just a hamburger, and move on.

All around the block Haruo looked in every shop. He was sure that his father wasn't nearby. He broke into a run. Perhaps he could eat a piece of pie if he hurried. That would be swell. A banana cream or pineapple. He mustn't forget to ask Nick about the flowers. Maybe some of his customers would also make purchases.

Breathlessly he ran in the cafe and carefully laid his packages in the corner. First he saw Nick, who broadly grinned at him. "Hello, young man!" he cried. "How are you?" Then he noticed his father sitting and facing him, his small gimlet eyes studying him with a sly smile. For a second Haruo stood open-mouthed and then backed away quickly to the corner to pick up the packages and run outside.

"Haruo!" cried his father, smiling and holding up his hand. "Haruo, come back here."

Haruo hesitated. His father was still sitting leisurely. He could get away easily. He could run out, hide, and never allow his father to touch him. There was danger in remaining. Still he hesitated.

"Come here, Haruo. How are you doing?" his father said. "Business good today?"

Haruo slowly approached his father. "I made seven dollars already," he said.

"Good! You're doing fine," his father said. "Sit down here, Haruo, and let's have lunch together."

"What'll you have, young man?" Nick asked.

Haruo sat down, looking cautiously at his father. "I want a hamburger and a banana cream pie," he said.

Nick went away to fill the order. His father looked in the corner.

"You still have some flowers to sell?" he asked.

Haruo nodded. "I have four bunches of carnations and three bunches of roses left."

"You sell them easily," his father said cheerfully. "Over seven dollars for the day. Not bad. I know you could earn it every day. You're pretty smart."

Nick came back with the order.

"Let's eat, Haruo," his father said. "I like Nick's hamburgers best. They're always good. How about you, Haruo?"

Haruo nodded his head while his mouth bit into the sandwich.

"I don't worry about you, Haruo," said his father. "No, sir. You can go out in the world today, and I know you can make a living. But your mama. She's worried about you. She wants you to come home. You don't want to worry her, Haruo."

Haruo sat silently munching his hamburger. He glanced at his father, who smiled back. Nick whistled and watched the hamburgers sizzle in the pans. A noon whistle went off at the factory several blocks away. Presently people cluttered in Nick's. All around him Haruo listened to the talk of business and of labor. He listened importantly to their talk and watched his banana cream disappear.

"Anything else, young man?" Nick asked him.

Haruo smiled and shook his head. His father got up and paid the bill.

"Come home when you're through selling the flowers. Mama will be expecting you," his father said. "I have to go home now and watch the store. You take your time, Haruo."

His father went away. Haruo sat sipping his milk and listened to the men talking of inflation, civil liberties, and sports. When he was finally through with his lunch Nick came over and bought a dozen carnations. "Goodbye, young man," were the departing words of Nick.

Outside Haruo walked up and down the main street carrying his packages without attempting to sell a bunch. The sun shone brightly. This was a swell day. A swell day to go to the ball park and see the Oaks and the Seals tangle. No, it was a greater day than that. He could leap, sing, and run all the way home. This was something he had never before experienced. This was a great thrill. Then he remembered his greatest disappointment, bitterness, and loneliness of last night as a prelude to joy. His warm laughing face became solemn. Suddenly tears filled his eyes. He wiped his tears with his sleeves and wondered if the people were noticing him in such a condition.

■ ■ ■

Boys

Anton Chekhov

In this story the great Russian writer Anton Chekhov (1860–1904) describes the antics and imaginary lives of two ten-year-old boys. Except for their names and speech, Volodya and his friend Lentilov could be boys from the neigborhoods of Local News— or from any neighborhood where young people dream of adventure.

"VOLODYA'S come!" someone shouted in the yard.

"Master Volodya's here!" bawled Natalya the cook, running into the dining-room. "Oh, my goodness!"

The whole Korolyov family, who had been expecting their Volodya from hour to hour, rushed to the windows. At the front door stood a wide sledge, with three white horses in a cloud of steam. The sledge was empty, for Volodya was already in the hall, untying his hood with red and chilly fingers. His school overcoat, his cap, his snowboots, and the hair on his temples were all white with frost, and his whole figure from head to foot diffused such a pleasant, fresh smell of the snow that the very sight of him made one want to shiver and say "brrr!"

His mother and aunt ran to kiss and hug him. Natalya plumped down at his feet and began pulling off his snowboots, his sisters shrieked with delight, the doors creaked and banged, and Volodya's father, in his waistcoat and shirt-sleeves, ran out into the hall with scissors in his hand, and cried out in alarm:

"We were expecting you all yesterday! Did you come all right? Had a good journey? Mercy on us! You might let him say 'how do you do' to his father! I am his father after all!"

"Bow-wow!" barked the huge black dog, Milord, in a deep bass, tapping with his tail on the walls and furniture. For two minutes there was nothing but a general hubbub of joy. After the first outburst of delight was over the Korolyovs noticed that there was, besides their Volodya, another small person in the hall, wrapped up in scarves and shawls and white with frost. He was standing perfectly still in a corner, in the shadow of a big fox-lined overcoat.

"Volodya darling, who is it?" asked his mother, in a whisper.

"Oh!" cried Volodya." This is—let me introduce my friend Lentilov, a schoolfellow in the second class[1]. . . . I have brought him to stay with us."

"Delighted to hear it! You are very welcome," the father said cordially. "Excuse me, I've been at work without my coat. . . . Please come in! Natalya, help Mr. Lentilov off with his things. Mercy on us, do turn that dog out! He is unendurable!"

A few minutes later, Volodya and his friend Lentilov, some-what dazed by their noisy welcome, and still red from the out-side cold, were sitting down to tea. The winter sun, making its way through the snow and the frozen tracery on the window-panes, gleamed on the samovar, and plunged its pure rays in the tea-basin. The room was warm, and the boys felt as though the warmth and the frost were struggling together with a tin-gling sensation in their bodies.

"Well, Christmas will soon be here," the father said in a pleasant sing-song voice, rolling a cigarette of dark reddish tobacco. "It doesn't seem long since the summer, when mamma was crying at your going . . . and here you are back again. . . . Time flies, my boy. Before you have time to cry out, old age is upon you. Mr. Lentilov, take some more, please help yourself! We don't stand on ceremony!"

Volodya's three sisters, Katya, Sonya, and Masha (the eldest was eleven), sat at the table and never took their eyes off the newcomer. Lentilov was of the same height and age as Volodya, but not as round-faced and fair-skinned. He was thin, dark, and freckled; his hair stood up like a brush, his eyes were small, and his lips were thick. He was, in fact, distinctly ugly, and if he had not been wearing the school uniform[2], he might have been

---

1. A grammar-school boy in the second class would be about ten years old.
2. All students in Czarist Russia wore uniforms.

taken for the son of a cook. He seemed morose, did not speak, and never once smiled. The little girls, staring at him, immediately came to the conclusion that he must be a very clever and learned person. He seemed to be thinking about something all the time, and was so absorbed in his own thoughts, that, whenever he was spoken to, he started, threw his head back, and asked to have the question repeated.

The little girls noticed that Volodya, who had always been so merry and talkative, also said very little, did not smile at all, and hardly seemed to be glad to be home. All the time they were at tea he only once addressed his sisters, and then he said something so strange. He pointed to the samovar and said:

"In California they don't drink tea, but gin."

He, too, seemed absorbed in his own thoughts, and, to judge by the looks that passed between him and his friend Lentilov, their thoughts were the same. After tea, they all went into the nursery. The girls and their father took up the work that had been interrupted by the arrival of the boys. They were making flowers and frills for the Christmas tree out of paper of different colours. It was an attractive and noisy occupation. Every fresh flower was greeted by the little girls with shrieks of delight, even of awe, as though the flower had dropped straight from heaven; their father was in ecstasies too, and every now and then he threw the scissors on the floor, in vexation at their bluntness. Their mother kept running into the nursery with an anxious face, asking:

"Who has taken my scissors? Ivan Nikolaitch, have you taken my scissors again?"

"Mercy on us! I'm not even allowed a pair of scissors!" their father would respond in a lachrymose voice, and, flinging himself back in his chair, he would pretend to be a deeply injured man; but a minute later, he would be in ecstasies again.

On his former holidays Volodya, too, had taken part in the preparations for the Christmas tree, or had been running in the yard to look at the snow mountain[3] that the watchman and the shepherd were building. But this time Volodya and Lentilov took no notice whatever of the coloured paper, and did not once go into the stable. They sat in the window and began whispering to one another; then they opened an atlas and looked carefully at a map.

"First to Perm . . ." Lentilov said, in an undertone, "from there to Tiumen, then Tomsk . . . then . . . then . . . Kamchatka. There the Samoyedes take one over Behring's Straits in boats. . . . And then we are in America. . . . There are lots of furry animals there. . . ."

"And California?" asked Volodya.

"California is lower down. . . . We've only to get to America and California is not far off. . . . And one can get a living by hunting and plunder."

All day long Lentilov avoided the little girls, and seemed to look at them with suspicion. In the evening he happened to be left alone with them for five minutes or so. It was awkward to be silent. He cleared his throat morosely, rubbed his left hand against his right, looked sullenly at Katya and asked:

"Have you read Mayne Reid[4]?"

"No, I haven't. . . . I say, can you skate?"

Absorbed in his own reflections, Lentilov made no reply to this question; he simply puffed out his cheeks, and gave a long sigh as though he were very hot. He looked up at Katya once more and said:

"When a herd of bisons stampedes across the prairie the earth trembles, and the frightened mustangs kick and neigh."

He smiled impressively and added:

"And the Indians attack the trains, too. But worst of all are the mosquitoes and the termites."

"Why, what's that?"

"They're something like ants, but with wings. They bite fearfully. Do you know who I am?"

---

3. A hill built of snow for the purpose of sledding.
4. Thomas Mayne Reid (1818–1883) wrote popular adventure stories for boys, mostly about the American West.

"Mr. Lentilov."

"No, I am Montehomo, the Hawk's Claw, Chief of the Ever Victorious."

Masha, the youngest, looked at him, then into the darkness out of window and said, wondering:

"And we had lentils for supper yesterday."

Lentilov's incomprehensible utterances, and the way he was always whispering with Volodya, and the way Volodya seemed now to be always thinking about something instead of playing . . . all this was strange and mysterious. And the two elder girls, Katya and Sonya, began to keep a sharp look-out on the boys. At night, when the boys had gone to bed, the girls crept to their bedroom door, and listened to what they were saying. Ah, what they discovered! The boys were planning to run away to America to dig for gold: they had everything ready for the journey, a pistol, two knives, biscuits, a burning glass to serve instead of matches, a compass, and four roubles in cash. They learned that the boys would have to walk some thousands of miles, and would have to fight tigers and savages on the road: then they would get gold and ivory, slay their enemies, become pirates, drink gin, and finally marry beautiful maidens, and make a plantation.

The boys interrupted each other in their excitement. Throughout the conversation, Lentilov called himself "Montehomo, the Hawk's Claw," and Volodya was "my pale-face brother!"

"Mind you don't tell mamma," said Katya, as they went back to bed. "Volodya will bring us gold and ivory from America, but if you tell mamma he won't be allowed to go."

The day before Christmas Eve, Lentilov spent the whole day poring over the map of Asia and making notes, while Volodya, with a languid and swollen face that looked as though it had been stung by a bee, walked about the rooms and ate nothing. And once he stood still before the holy image in the nursery, crossed himself, and said:

"Lord, forgive me a sinner; Lord, have pity on my poor unhappy mamma!"

In the evening he burst out crying. On saying good-night he gave his father a long hug, and then hugged his mother and sisters. Katya and Sonya knew what was the matter, but little Masha was puzzled, completely puzzled. Every time she looked at Lentilov she grew thoughtful and said with a sigh:

"When Lent comes, nurse says we shall have to eat peas and lentils."

Early in the morning of Christmas Eve, Katya and Sonya slipped quietly out of bed, and went to find out how the boys meant to run away to America. They crept to their door.

"Then you don't mean to go?" Lentilov was saying angrily. "Speak out: aren't you going?"

"Oh dear," Volodya wept softly. "How can I go? I feel so unhappy about mamma."

"My pale-face brother, I pray you, let us set off. You declared you were going, you egged me on, and now the time comes, you funk it[5]!"

"I . . . I . . . I'm not funking it, but I . . . I . . . I'm sorry for mamma."

"Say once and for all, are you going or are you not?"

"I am going, only . . . wait a little . . . I want to be at home a little."

"In that case I will go by myself," Lentilov declared. "I can get on without you. And you wanted to hunt tigers and fight! Since that's how it is, give me back my cartridges!"

At this Volodya cried so bitterly that his sisters could not help crying too. Silence followed.

"So you are not coming?" Lentilov began again.

"I . . . I . . . I am coming!"

"Well, put on your things, then."

And Lentilov tried to cheer Volodya up by singing the praises of America, growling like a tiger, pretending to be a

---

5. The American slang expression would be "chicken out" (act in a cowardly manner).

steamer, scolding him, and promising to give him all the ivory and lions' and tigers' skins.

And this thin, dark boy, with his freckles and his bristling shock of hair, impressed the little girls as an extraordinary remarkable person. He was a hero, a determined character, who knew no fear, and he growled so ferociously, that, standing at the door, they really might imagine there was a tiger or lion inside. When the little girls went back to their room and dressed, Katya's eyes were full of tears, and she said:

"Oh, I feel so frightened!"

Everything was as usual till two o'clock, when they sat down to dinner. Then it appeared that the boys were not in the house. They sent to the servants' quarters, to the stables, to the bailiff's cottage. They were not to be found. They sent into the village—they were not there. At tea, too, the boys were still absent, and by supper-time Volodya's mother was dreadfully uneasy, and even shed tears. Late in the evening they sent again to the village, they searched everywhere, and walked along the river bank with lanterns. Heavens! what a fuss there was!

Next day the police officer came, and a paper of some sort was written out in the dining-room. Their mother cried. . . .

All of a sudden a sledge stopped at the door, with three white horses in a cloud of steam.

"Volodya's come," someone shouted in the yard.

"Master Volodya's here!" bawled Natalya, running into the dining-room. And Milord barked his deep bass, "bow-wow."

It seemed that the boys had been stopped in the Arcade, where they had gone from shop to shop asking where they could get gunpowder. Volodya burst into sobs as soon as he came into the hall, and flung himself on his mother's neck. The little girls, trembling, wondered with terror what would happen next. They saw their father take Volodya and Lentilov into his study, and there he talked to them a long while.

"Is this a proper thing to do?" their father said to them. "I only pray they won't hear of it at school, you would both be expelled. You ought to be ashamed, Mr. Lentilov, really. It's not at all the thing to do! You began it, and I hope you will be punished by your parents. How could you? Where did you spend the night?"

"At the station," Lentilov answered proudly.

Then Volodya went to bed, and had a compress, steeped in vinegar, on his forehead. A telegram was sent off, and next day a lady, Lentilov's mother, made her appearance and bore off her son. Lentilov looked morose and haughty to the end, and he did not utter a single word at taking leave of the little girls. But he took Katya's book and wrote in it as a souvenir: "Montehomo, the Hawk's Claw, Chief of the Ever Victorious."

■ ■ ■

Gary Soto
(1952–)

Because Gary Soto had few books around when he was growing up and little encouragement to read, he was not planning to
become an author. Instead, he thought about being lots of other
things: a priest, a barber, or maybe a scientist who studies
dinosaurs. In fact, he went to college to become a geographer.
But when he found a book of poetry in the college library, he
was drawn to it. Reading the poetry inside changed his life and
inspired him to become an author himself.

Soto writes poetry, novels, and stories for adults and children.
He writes about what he knows, mainly what it is like to be a
Mexican American boy growing up poor in central California.
Soto often writes about enjoyable childhood experiences, but
his life was also filled with hardship. He was born on April 12,
1952, in Fresno, which is in the heavily agricultural San Joaquin
Valley. His grandparents were born in Mexico. Both his parents
and grandparents worked as laborers in the fields and factories
around Fresno. They picked oranges, grapes, and cotton. Soto
himself grew up doing physical labor. He picked grapes, washed
cars, mowed lawns, and painted house numbers on curbs.

When Soto was five, he moved with his family to a
Mexican American neighborhood, or *barrio,* on the edge of
Fresno. Tragedy struck the family not long after their move,
however. Soto's father was killed in an accident at the factory
where he worked; he was only twenty seven years old. Soto's
mother had to raise her children alone. They grew up very poor.
All of these experiences—living in the *barrio,* losing his father,
being poor—show up in different ways in Soto's stories, poems,
and plays.

Although Soto sometimes gets his ideas from the experiences
of others, most of his stories and poems are the products of his

own imagination and life experience. To create a believable picture of what it was like to grow up in the *barrio* in Fresno, Soto draws heavily upon his own childhood memories. But the way he carefully blends all of these elements together—the memories of his own childhood, ideas from his imagination, and the experiences of other people—can make it difficult for readers to tell which parts of his stories and poems are autobiographical and which are not.

■ ■ ■